ML.

STO

DETECTIVE STORIES

DEAD MARCH IN THREE KEYS

Norah Lofts writes:

One day in 1938, in the middle of a jocular conversation I said, "If anybody did that to me, I should die!" And I thought—There would be no clue, no mark, nothing. The perfect murder. I kept thinking about it, shaping up the characters and the circumstances and then I wrote DEAD MARCH IN THREE KEYS. When it was finished I asked our local Chief Constable to read it and answer the question, "What could the Police do?" He replied, laconically, "Nothing." But in 1938 society was less permissive and in books and films murderers were not supposed to go unpunished; so I had to write the whole thing again, carefully planting the *psychological* clues that would prove to be the murderer's undoing.

The trouble was that I had already published two or three period novels—not very successfully—and I felt that to pick up a book by Norah Lofts and find that it was a crime story would disappoint my readers—both of them! So because my publisher was Peter Davies and my agent Curtis Brown, that book went out under the name of Peter Curtis. Since then, from time to time, by way of relaxation, I have lent my typewriter to PC who produced YOU'RE BEST ALONE—filmed as GUILT IS MY SHADOW, LADY LIVING ALONE and THE LITTLE WAX DOLL. It was a proud day for PC when one of his books was translated into Hebrew, a thing which had never happened to NL. Actually I intended to preserve the pseudonym forever, but there was a leak somewhere; and since, over the years NL had monopolised the typewriter, increasing her output and gaining a few more readers, it seemed good policy to re-issue the books in her name. Always with the fervent hope that no reader will suffer the disappointment which the pseudonym was devised to avoid.

Also by Norah Lofts:

Bless This House
The Brittle Glass
Out of This Nettle
Silver Nutmeg
To See a Fine Lady
A Calf for Venus
The Devil in Clevely
(Afternoon of an Autocrat)
Jassy
Queen in Waiting
The Road to Revelation
Heaven in Your Hand
The Town House
The House at Old Vine
The House at Sunset
Scent of Cloves
The Lute Player
The Concubine
How Far to Bethlehem?
Hester Roon
The Little Wax Doll

Dead March in Three Keys

NORAH LOFTS

HODDER AND STOUGHTON

1800372

Emma Plume

I HAD my first suspicion the moment I read that letter. Mind, I don't mean that I had any idea what had happened, or that I had any idea of the awful truth, but I did feel uneasy and unhappy; and as I took off my reading glasses and laid them down on the open page I asked myself, 'Well, what is *he* up to now? And why did she ever let him write to me like that?'

On the face of it, the letter, written in his beautiful flowing hand, was plausible and reasonable enough.

Dear Nanny,

As you will see we are now comfortably installed in the new house. Mrs. Curwen has stood the move surprisingly well but she is rather tired and that is why I am writing for her. While you and Diana have been away we have been talking about our arrangements for her future. We find that this village is inconveniently distant from any school which she could attend and have come to the conclusion that we must provide her with a governess. It is, anyway, time she dispensed with a nurse.

Reluctant therefore as we are to relinquish your services, we have decided that the break had better be made at the

11

end of this holiday and that it would be as well, for the child's sake, that you do not return with her. As you know she is much attached to you and we feel that this regrettable but necessary change will be more acceptable if it coincides with her coming to a new house with a good many things to distract her attention in the first few days.

With this in mind I have arranged that the governess shall take over from you at Hunstanton on the morning of the 29th when the holiday ends. She will come from London and should be in Hunstanton by a quarter to one. She will call at the lodgings, collect the child and the luggage and catch the one-ten to Colchester which is a restaurant train and they can lunch on it. I have given her minute instructions as to the journey and have tried to arrange everything to give you the least possible trouble.

Mrs. Curwen expresses a wish that you should not tell Diana that you are leaving her for good. Tell her that you are going to take a little holiday on your own. We will break the news to her ourselves.

Your trunk and the black box are being sent on to you.

The enclosed cheque is a small token of our esteem and best wishes and I need hardly say that if you should ever wish for a testimonial we shall be only too glad to tell the world what a treasure we have had in you.

Finally we wish to thank you for all your care and affection for Diana, especially in her illness.

Mrs. Curwen sends her love and joins me in all good wishes.

Yours sincerely,
Richard Curwen.

A pleasant, plausible letter: and the cheque—for fifty pounds—was generous. I was forced to admit, too, that all he said about a governess was true. Miss Diana would be six in October, and though she knew her letters and could count a little, I was forced to own that I was no great shakes as a teacher.

No, the manner of my dismissal left little to be desired —except that it prevented me from seeing Miss Eloise to say good-bye to her. It was the fact that I had been dismissed at all which puzzled me and made me uneasy.

I had been with Miss Eloise (as she remained to me, in my mind and on my tongue, though she had been Mrs. Curwen these seven years) since I was twenty and she a girl of twelve. I had nursed and tended her since the dreadful day when her mother died and she had taken the first of those hysterical fits which no doctor and no treatment had seemed able to cure. She had said to me over and over again, 'What should I do without you, Nanny? Don't ever leave me, will you? Promise?' And I, like a fool, had promised and kept to it. Hadn't I refused Michael O'Hara, who was the breath of my body, because he was going to Canada and wouldn't consider coming into the house and driving the car and sharing Miss Eloise's service?

And lately, how many times lately had Miss Eloise said to me, 'When Miss Diana does go to school, Nanny, I shall have you all to myself again. And nobody looks after me as you do.' And that *was* true. You have to really love a person in order to have the patience and the skill which I had cultivated during all those years.

And now, there I was, thrown off at a moment's notice. There'd not been a word of this spoken when I came away from the Chimney House in July to spend the summer with Miss Diana at the sea. It was all so sudden, and I hate sudden things.

It was *his* doing, and I couldn't think why. It wasn't that he was jealous. He never wanted to do anything for his wife when she was ill or in a frenzy. Oh no. He'd just stand and watch as if he was at a theatre show and then he would call for me. I knew he hated me, but then he'd hated me for

13

seven years without doing anything about it. *How* had he persuaded her to let him write that letter? 'There's some hokey-pokey somewhere,' I said to myself.

Miss Diana came and put her little hand on my knee to attract my attention. 'Is that a letter from Mummy?' she asked. 'What about the little donkey?'

I remembered the donkey with a start of surprise.

'Well, no, dearie, there's no letter from your Mummy, and Daddy hasn't mentioned the donkey at all.'

Her bright face clouded and her lower lip came out in a way that showed that tears were not far off. So I said hastily, 'Perhaps there'll be another letter, later on. The postman comes twice a day here, you know.'

The business about the donkey had begun a few days earlier when she was taking her daily ride on the beach. The weather had broken, it was getting towards the end of September, and the holiday season was ending. For once there were more donkeys than children and we did not have to wait, as we so often had had to do, for Miss Diana to be able to choose her favourite, a very small donkey, named, because of his dirty white colour, Snowball.

I lifted her down when the ride was ended and as I did so she said to the man, 'Snowball will have *his* holiday now, won't he?'

'Well, no, Miss. This is his holiday in a manner of speaking. I can't keep six mokes eating their heads off all winter. Snowball'll be pulling a vegetable cart next week.'

'He's too little,' said the child, smiling in frank disbelief as she offered the animal the carrot that was part of the routine.

' 'Swonderful what even a little donkey'll pull with Ben Meadows behind him,' said the man.

From that moment I got no peace at all. Miss Diana, who was in many ways precocious and imaginative and had

14

her mother's tender heart for all dumb things, got firmly into her head that the donkey was doomed to pull a wagon and that Ben Meadows, a big, brutal man, would ride behind with a stick. Nothing would do but that Snowball must be bought and taken home with her.

It did not seem an impossible thing. The new house into which Mr. and Mrs. Curwen were moving had a good deal of ground and was near the sea. It would be better than a daily walk for giving the child an airing if she could continue her daily donkey ride and make it last as long as she wished. A donkey of that size would take very little to keep it. Beyond all, I knew that Miss Eloise would be all in favour of the scheme, not to mention her reluctance to refuse the child anything within reason.

So I had written myself, explaining all about the animal, and guided Miss Diana's hand through a special appeal of her own, and as I wrote the address on the envelope I thought that my next letter would go to Moat Place, not to the Chimney House. I was rather sorry about the move, the new house sounded very far away from everywhere and the sea only appeals to me for a very short time in the height of the summer. I hadn't fancied the idea of living by it in November, or in March. Well, I needn't have worried myself about that. Moat House was not going to see me.

'Do you think Mummy has forgotten about Snowball?' Miss Diana insisted.

'No,' I said. 'That's not the kind of thing your mother is likely to forget. We shall hear, you'll see, later on.'

And at that moment I was quite sure that I should get word from the mistress herself. She would never let me go without that much. And probably, I thought, she hadn't mentioned the donkey to the master, wanting it to be a matter between herself and the child. I shouldn't have gone to him about a donkey's troubles, myself. His own

15

happiness and comfort were all that he cared about: that was the chief thing I had against him. That and his affair with Miss Antonia.

We waited two days more, but no word came from the mistress, though my trunk, which I had left at the Chimney House to be moved with all the other things to Moat Place, was sent on to the lodgings. When I took it in and asked the landlady to let it stand somewhere on the ground floor I looked at it and felt that my last link with Miss Eloise had broken. That and not hearing made me feel anxious and I wondered whether the move had been too much for her and she was having one of her attacks. The trunk's arrival though did help me over the breaking of the news of my going to Miss Diana. She asked why it had been sent—she was a great one for asking questions—and I replied that it contained things that I needed on my holiday. She was a little surprised to learn that I was going off by myself, but took it calmly, thank Heaven, after asking whether she had to go in the train alone. I explained that a lady was coming specially to look after her and that she would then teach her to write properly so that next holiday she would be able to write letters to her mother for herself, and she seemed to quite take to that idea, too.

But about the donkey she would not be content. It got to the 27th and on that day she was completely out of hand. She refused her food, insisted upon remaining in sight of the donkey-stand all day, ran after every postman she saw, wept for the slightest thing and was, in short, as difficult as only she knew how to be. In the end, just to quieten her I went to the Post Office and sent a telegram.

PLEASE INSTRUCT ABOUT DONKEY. MISS DIANA MUCH UPSET.

I sent it to *her*, specially. The answer came back from *him*.

16

MRS. CURWEN IN BED, EXHAUSTED. NOTHING SERIOUS. PLEASE YOURSELF.

In the light of later events I could see that the most significant words there were 'Nothing serious.' If there had been the slightest hint that anything was seriously wrong with Miss Eloise I should have been at Moat Place like a homing pigeon, sacked or not. As it was, however, I thought that the exhaustion was only to be expected; she should never have tried to be present at a house-moving. She should have come away with me and the child as I had suggested. And if I went storming back after being dismissed by him there would only have been another of those hateful scenes which exhausted her more than anything else.

I did see from the telegram that she hadn't mentioned the donkey to him. That was plain. One doesn't telegraph to nurses, and dismissed nurses at that, that they are to please themselves about buying a donkey.

However, I did please myself. I told Miss Diana that if she would eat at least three pieces of bread and butter for her tea we would go and buy the donkey at once. I had drawn five pounds out of my Post Office for my fare to London and expenses there, on the day that I had received the letter. But I reckoned that I had just enough without that and could wait until I got there before taking any more.

So we went down to the donkey-stand and bought Snowball for four pounds ten and arranged that he was to be sent to the nearest station to Moat Place, a place called Notham St. Mary. I said that the carriage would be paid there; and that it would be convenient if the animal could arrive on the 29th because then the master could arrange about getting it home while he was at the station meeting Miss Diana and the governess. The donkey man seemed capable

17

and sensible and promised that he would attend to everything.

Miss Diana was in a transport of delight. She threw her arms round the donkey's neck and promised him everything that a child's mind could suggest of luxury, comfort and pleasure. There was just one more dangerous moment. As we were leaving the place she said, 'What about the others?' I tipped the donkey man a wink and said, 'All the rest are going to live in a big meadow.'

He understood and said: 'That's right, Missie. The others are going out to grass.'

We spent the next day visiting Snowball and buying little presents for her to take home. Now that the time for parting was drawing so near I began to feel very down in the mouth. After all, I'd had Miss Diana from the very start and she was the sweetest child imaginable. I'd not known Miss Eloise as a small child: she was twelve when I went as under-nursemaid to her young brother who died in infancy, but I always thought that I could see the very young Miss Eloise in her daughter and several times had taken pleasure in the fact that there was nothing of *him* in her at all.

But feel as I might, I was in duty bound to keep a bright face before Miss Diana. She thought I was just going to take a little holiday and would soon be with her again. And I think that the effort to control myself did me good. Crying never helped anybody yet: so though at times I felt I wanted to take her in my arms and cry and cry my heart out, I was forced to smile and talk about Snowball and the good times we would all have together in the new house.

The evening that I was dreading came at last. I gave her the last bath, heard her short evening prayer for the last time, saw her into bed and watched her fall asleep. Then I began to pack, a job which I had put off because I wanted

18

to give her the whole of my attention during the last few hours. My heart grew more and more sore and leaden. I still had had no word from Miss Eloise and I thought somehow he'd managed, after all these years, to turn her against me. Said something about how I was crusty and set in my ways, perhaps, and gone over again the little rumpus that I had had with Woods, the parlourmaid.

Despite my resolution I did fold away several tears amongst the little dresses and coats and shoes. And then my attention was distracted. The landlady came to say that there was a lady, a Miss Duffield, to see me. I'd never heard the name before and went downstairs rather dubiously. In the sitting-room where Miss Diana and I had taken our meals there was a stranger, a young woman of about eight and twenty with a nice bright sensible face and a pleasant manner.

She told me that she was the governess whom Mr. Curwen had engaged for his child.

'I was supposed to pick her up here tomorrow at about a quarter to one, but that meant getting up very early. Also, when I was a child I once had a lovely holiday in this place, and I've never seen it since. I thought, since I was coming, I might as well come tonight and have a look round in the morning. It doesn't make any difference, does it? The woman says I can have a room here.'

'I'm very glad to see you,' I said, and that was indeed the truth. I was very glad to be able to have a look at the person to whom I was to resign my charge, and pleased to see that she was young enough to be lively and yet not just a silly bit of a girl.

'Take your things off,' I said. 'I expect you'd like some supper. I was going to have mine in a minute. Do you mind sharing it?'

'I'd be glad to,' she said. She took off her nice tweed coat and hung it on the back of a chair. She had on a good blouse, and I always think that you can tell a lady by her blouse, I don't know why, but I do know that I've never seen a nasty woman in a nice blouse yet. Her shoes and gloves and her handbag were neat and good, too, and altogether she impressed me very favourably.

There is, always has been and I suppose always will be, a kind of underground warfare between nurses and governesses. To begin with, the nurses resent handing over the children to somebody else and the governesses are a little jealous of the regard and affection which children feel for their Nannies. Then they look at the same child from such a very different point of view. The nurse wants a child to grow and be healthy. The governess wants it to learn and be a credit to her. Sometimes these wants clash. Also, there is a social difference between the two. Most nurses are sensible women of the working-class, with no pretensions. (I am not reckoning those young females with badges and uniforms who are always talking about vitamins and calories and saying what a good time they had in college, just to let you know they've been.) But the governesses are mostly jumped-up young hussies, afraid to be civil, in case they 'lose caste,' as they call it, when you want them to take an odd meal with the staff in an emergency; or else broken-down ladies, full of memories of their better days, who don't know enough, or are too proud, to take a job in a proper school, where, I am told, the wages are enormous.

Bearing all this in mind, I was careful to ask Miss Duffield if she minded sharing my supper, and I kept my distance at the beginning of the meal. But she chatted away and seemed disposed to be friendly, and I was never one to throw back friendliness in anyone's face. When we had finished eating and were sitting over our last cups of tea, she opened her bag and offered me a cigarette.

Now, next to a cup of tea I did enjoy a cigarette more than anything, though I always have a feeling of guiltiness whenever I do smoke one. I had started the habit in rather a funny way. Miss Eloise made me. Just after she lost her father—that was in Birmingham in the good days before she met Mr. Curwen—she had a bad spell of sleeplessness and general bad nervous health. She was prone to that. But one day I discovered to my horror that she was taking some tablets, horrible things that made her sleep heavily and wake up without any life at all. They came from Germany and were sheer poison. I went for her in a way that no one else dared to. And then, just to show that I wasn't really unsympathetic, I said, 'Why don't you sometimes smoke a cigarette? Lots of ladies do nowadays, and they say they're good for the nerves. And really ladies do seem not to have the nerve-storms and hysteric fits that they used.'

And she, to show that she had forgiven my plain speaking, said, 'All right, Nanny. I will if you will. Let's start now. Send Parkes to buy some.'

At first we coughed and spluttered and said we couldn't see what people got out of it, but soon we knew and many's the cigarette we've had together. Though even so I never got over the feeling that I was doing something I shouldn't.

However, on this evening I accepted one of Miss Duffield's Player's, and since the evening had grown chilly I lighted the gas-fire and we drew our chairs near it. Sitting like that and smoking together made us feel friendly, and when she turned back her skirt and showed her nice slim legs and said: 'Now, if you don't mind, tell me something about the child's temperament. It would be such a help,' I felt my heart really warm to her. So few of them would have asked that, or would have been willing to admit that a nurse knew anything about a child apart from its stomach. I spent the happiest hour that I had had since the arrival of that letter in telling her about Miss Diana's funny little ways, how she never sulked or fretted unless there really was something wrong. How slapping and scolding were worse than useless, and how only that spring a mere common cold had turned into a serious illness for her and that she shouldn't be overworked or worried, or above all allowed to go out improperly clad or keep on anything that was the least bit damp. They were all the things that I had longed to say and didn't ever dream I would get a chance to say to the right person.

And that Miss Duffield was the right person I grew, moment by moment, more assured. She listened, she didn't just pretend to, and now and then she would murmur, 'That's interesting,' or 'I must remember that.' At last I had told her everything that I could think of. She looked at the clock, reached out and found her cigarettes and held them towards me. 'No, no,' I said, 'you must have one of mine.' I found my packet and offered it.

'My word,' she said, 'you treat yourself well. Passing Clouds, indeed. Very plutocratic.'

'Miss Eloise keeps me in cigarettes,' I said. 'She always has done, since the time we began smoking together.'

'And who is she?' she asked. 'An elder daughter?'

'Good gracious no. That's Mrs. Curwen's name, but somehow it comes natural to me to call her by her old name.'

I didn't know much of what they call psychology, but I had enough of what the Bible calls 'knowing thyself' to know that I hated the name Curwen because it was his; and that was really at the bottom of my sticking to the old name.

'I see,' she said. 'Now, if you aren't in a hurry to get to bed, I would like you just to tell me a few things about the parents as well. You've shown me how very observant you are, by your description of the child. You might save me from making mistakes, you know, by telling me a little about them. Not gossipy things, just what they're like, what they like and what they don't. You know . . .'

Now all the time I had been talking about Miss Diana, I had had at the back of my mind the thought that I would like to put in a word for Miss Eloise. For ever since I had seen that the governess was young and quite pretty I had thought, 'He'll fuss round her, like he did round Woods and several other people, and that'll be one more in the house on *his* side and one less on *hers*.' And that might lead to trouble, especially as the governess was dealing with the child, whom Miss Eloise loved and he didn't really care a rap about in his heart. And I knew, though I hated to admit it, that a stranger coming into the house might think the mistress queer and unimportant, while the master could be completely charming if he wanted to, and could always seem to have reason on his side, especially as, in an upset, Miss Eloise always lost her head and cried or fainted and acted a bit strange. So I chose my words very carefully and now and then paused and took my time, getting up to ask the landlady for a pot of tea and to listen to Miss Diana's sleeping breath, just to give myself time to think how much to say and how best to say it. I had to remember that, though I liked the girl, she was a stranger to me.

'You couldn't have asked a better person,' I began, 'for I have known Mrs. Curwen since she was twelve and I've known her husband for as long as she has. Mrs. Curwen is the sweetest person I've ever met, and I don't mean all coo-ey and lovey-dovey. But she needs understanding. No, no, I don't mean by that that she's fratchety or unreliable . . . but you may meet her when she isn't very well—as a matter of fact she is in bed now—and then you might think that she was dull and silly and that *he* has all the charm. I'd better tell you the whole story because if not you may get some garbled account from somebody else. But mind, this is confidential.

'When Miss Eloise was nearly twelve her brother was born. Her parents were very pleased because they had wanted a boy and given up all hope of having one. I went into the nursery then, as under-nursemaid. The child died; it was nobody's fault, but his mother took the notion that it was because she hadn't been able to feed him herself. She was a very sensitive and highly strung lady and it preyed on her poor mind. She killed herself. She couldn't have been in her right mind or she would never have done it, at least not the way she did, right in front of Miss Eloise when they were out together. They crossed the line in front of a train and she pushed the child away up the bank and then ran back and lay down. Of course we tried to make out that it was an accident, but I never thought that Miss Eloise believed a word of it. She said once, "But she wanted it to happen, she lay down." She was ill for a long time after that, nothing definite, just nervous trouble, and who should wonder, and she was never the same again. A sudden noise, a bad dream, a difference of opinion that no one else would think twice over just drives her either frantic or into a kind of stupor. Badly balanced, that's the term they use, I believe.

'She's very well off, but she has never lived like a person of means. She hates people. She just loves her garden and her pets and a very few people. She is passionately devoted to the child, though she tries hard not to be possessive or to let the child grow up with nerves. She's very, very kind-hearted, I've never known her to hurt a thing. She'll have a drowning spider lifted out of the bath with a loofah and put on the window-sill. Any kind of cruelty or violence upsets her more than a murder would most people. You want to be careful what you say to her, never tell her about an accident—or repeat any supernatural story to her. Mind that. Once, a long time ago, while they were still entertaining a few people now and then, a man at the dinner-table said that he was psychic—is that the word?—and told a story to prove it. She fainted dead away. My, there was a

24

confusion. We thought we'd never get her round. She wasn't herself for days. But if you are kind and reasonable with her, and show that you take an interest in the child, and treat her as though all her funny little ways didn't mean anything—why, then, you'll have a friend for life.'

'I see,' she said. 'Thank you for telling me. And what about the husband?'

'Oh, you'll like him,' I said. 'You'll think that he's the most charming and handsome man you've ever laid eyes on. You'll probably pity him because he's married to her. At least, that's the general opinion.'

'But not yours?' It was here that I took a walk to see to Miss Diana. By the time I came downstairs again I had decided that I might as well tell her.

'No. It's not mine. I've nothing very definite against him. You might not have anything very definite against a rough, handsome child that you saw clawing up a lot of snowdrops by the roots, or banging on a piano with boxing gloves on—but if you loved snowdrops, and had a feeling for the piano . . . Is that plain enough?'

Miss Duffield lit another cigarette before she answered.

'It's quite plain to me,' she said, 'that you much prefer Mrs. Curwen to Mr. Isn't that right?'

'I suppose so,' I said. 'And so, I wager, would any sensible person. But there are so few of them about. I was half hoping that you might be one.'

'We shall see. Now, tell me about the house.'

'That I can't do. I've never seen it. They've just moved into this one. Moat Place it's called, but you know that. It's very out of the way, I hope you don't mind that. But I believe it is a very nice house, set in lovely grounds. I think it sounds the sort of place that she would like.'

'Are you very sorry not to be going there?'

'In a way I am. But not for the sake of the house. I'm very sorry to be leaving Mrs. Curwen.'

'And why are you? Or is that a rude question?'

'It's the obvious one after I admit that I'm sorry to be leaving, isn't it? You see, Miss Diana is six now, she doesn't really need a nurse any more and there are no other children. Besides, I like them when they are very little indeed. I answered an advertisement in the paper the other day and I have an interview early next week with a lady who has twins of two and a half and a month-old baby.'

'They'll keep you busy,' she said smiling. And then, as though to close the conversation, she said, 'I can't tell you how much I appreciate all that you've told me. The Curwens won't seem like strangers at all. And I won't let Mr. Curwen's charm swamp me, I assure you.'

I looked at her, at her bright, sensible little face and sturdy upright figure, and I said, 'Somehow I don't think you will. There's just one thing you might do for me though. If you ever find the time you might just drop me a line and tell me how everything is getting on. I can't pretend that I shan't miss both Miss Eloise and Miss Diana very badly. Eighteen years is a long time and there's hardly a day in all that time when she hasn't wanted me to do something for her—Miss Eloise, I mean. I'm going to feel like an old hen that has lost its one chick, that I am.' There was no need to pretend in front of this grown woman, and suddenly the lump that I had been swallowing out of my throat all these days rose again and choked me. I put my head down on my arms and cried as though I were a baby.

She was very kind and sympathetic, gave me her handkerchief and patted my shoulder. After a bit I got control of myself again and sat up. I said, 'I'm sorry to make such a fool of myself.'

'Mrs. Curwen must have known how you felt about her,' she said thoughtfully. 'I wonder she could let you go.'

I forgot to be careful at that. 'I wonder too,' I gulped. 'That's what really is worrying me. But it isn't her doing, that I will swear. It's him. He's always trying to upset things and no doubt he has bawled about the expense of keeping an unnecessary servant. And it's all her money at that.'

'Is that so?' asked Miss Duffield, folding her arms. 'Tell me one thing more. Apparently he married her for her money. Is she very plain?'

'Indeed she is not,' I said hotly. 'I never saw but one woman who had her beat for looks and that was her own cousin, Antonia. She was supposed to be the handsomest, but times you could hardly tell 'em apart.'

Soon after that I went to bed. In the morning there was the last of the packing to do, the taxi to order and the child to console. I had little further speech with Miss Duffield and no time at all for thought. I gave her my sister's address in London and told her that any letter sent there would find me but that I would let her know as soon as I had settled in a new place.

'I'll be sure to write to you,' she promised. 'And you must write to me too. I shall be glad to have a letter. I haven't any people to write me, and you don't make many friends in my job. It's a lonely life in a way.'

I suddenly remembered something.

'Don't tell Miss Diana that I'm not coming back,' I said. 'She's thinking that I am going on a holiday. When she gets used to you, she won't mind so much.'

'I'll try to break it to her gently. And I don't think that I shall mention having met you, unless I have to. If he's set against you, as you seem to think, he might take exception to some of the things that I'll try to do as you told me. If he thinks they're my own ideas he'll probably think how right you were.'

'And try to look after Miss Eloise for me a little,' I pleaded, forgetting, in that last hour, that I ought still to feel rather hurt and sore with her. 'I'll be happier if I know that you're keeping an eye on her. Pander to her a bit, if you can.'

'I'll do my best,' she said, smiling; and somehow I felt that she would.

I went with them to the station. Miss Diana cried a little when the moment of parting actually came; and it was hard to comfort her without really telling a lie. She wished me a happy holiday so sweetly that tears came into my eyes again. I blinked them back, and waved and waved with a smile on my face until the train rounded the bend out of sight. Then I turned away. I had quite a lot to think about.

Richard Curwen

Once Nanny's letter had been composed and posted I felt easy in my mind. They say that every plan has one weak point and that every planner forgets something. So when I had been reminded of Emma Plume's existence and the imminence of her return and had dealt with that, I felt safe and happy.

Nevertheless I was shocked to find that it had been possible to overlook so important and dangerous a matter and I spent quite a long time going through the whole business again to assure myself that all was now well.

It began when I met Antonia. I know that people talk very wisely about the attraction of opposites: it may exist, for all I know, but I have always found that the people I like best are the people who are most like me. And Antonia was so like me in all essential things that our gravitation was as natural and inevitable as the gravitation of two particles of quicksilver.

Like me, Antonia lived by her looks and by her wits. Like me, she knocked up a living by various means. Sometimes she modelled dresses, sometimes sat for advertising photographs, earned a guinea or two as an extra in a film (good wardrobe essential), sold hats, worked in a teashop, kept house for somebody for six months, and so on. None of her jobs lasted long because—again like me—she had an incurable aversion to hard work and was easily bored by monotony. Her nature was luxurious and comfort-loving and her temper unreliable. If she felt like staying in bed, she stayed; if the weather were inclement she refused to face it; if she met with a reprimand she back-answered and walked out. And she was pretty and vital enough and had sufficient charm to be able to give rein to her whims without courting actual disaster.

She was very pretty. The best-looking woman I know, I used to tell myself gloatingly. She had marvellous coppery-red hair, clear grey eyes with black lashes, a flawless skin. Her figure was almost perfect too, broad enough at the shoulder, slim at the waist; and she moved well with an erectness and spring that belied her indolent nature.

She had a lively wit, a sprightly tongue and more intelligence than she cared to use. And even without these advantages she had a charm that comes from being easygoing, not over-virtuous, tolerant and out for a good time.

I fell in love with her at our first meeting. I had had affairs before. Since coming down from Oxford and learning that all my patrimony had been expended upon my so-called 'education' I had lived the masculine version of Antonia's own life and it had frequently paid me to engage in a little superficial love-making. Occasionally these affairs had grown more serious; but until I met her I had never seen a woman whom I wanted to marry for her own sake. Of course, there was not the slightest hope of my marrying Antonia. She made no bones about the fact that she intended to marry for money and had nothing but the most transient interest to give a young man who had no wealth, no prospects and nothing but his looks to commend him. We met, we came together and found that we had so many tastes and ideas and desires in common that we were immediately at home with one another. But we parted just as inevitably—she to go to a place in the country called Leet Hall where she was going to keep house for a rich old fellow named Meekin, and I to drag a backward, surly lout of a boy around the capitals and show-places of Europe.

When I came back I returned to my pied-à-terre in London, spent the cheque I had received for my exertions and then began to look around for another job. I was surprised and delighted to receive a letter from Antonia. It was as laconic as all her communications. 'Dear Dickon, do you think you could catalogue a library? (Not very difficult since its owner can barely read!) If so, ask Cecil to write to Joshua Meekin, address above, offering your services. Don't mention me. You don't know me. I'll explain why. Think I'm on a good thing here and hope to see you. Antonia.'

Cecil wrote, as requested, and within ten days I was installed at Leet Hall, trying to bring some sort of order into a vast and heterogeneous swarm of books which Joshua Meekin had acquired because he imagined that all country gentlemen owned libraries.

It did not need much explanation from Antonia to make the position quite clear to me. Joshua Meekin was paying in the usual coin for employing a young, attractive and unattached female to keep his house. He was falling in love with Antonia with all the exaggerated, humourless force that a hard-bitten fellow of fifty-five can bring to such a business. If he had known of the connection between Antonia and me he would never have had me in the house; and if he had known how rapidly and happily we got back on to the old footing he would have had me out of it promptly. But Antonia was clever, and he never knew; though I have no doubt that my presence about the place and my hardly concealed admiration for her helped her to pull off that little job. For although her employer was de-

c

finitely in love with her he had hesitated before making what Antonia referred to as an 'honourable proposal.'

'Of course, the other kind has its points,' she confessed. 'He's rich and pretty generous and might rise to a flat in town. But I shan't bate my price until I'm certain that I can't see Leet Hall through a leetle golden ring. In any case, waiting won't hurt him.'

So I worked very slowly at the library and Antonia worked at Joshua's final undoing, and now and then he caught us together and was obviously jealous, and before the cataloguing was finished he came across with his honourable proposal and Antonia was packed off to a friend in the village, a Mrs. Campbell, to remain virtuously under a neutral roof while the trousseau and the wedding feast could be prepared. Joshua's triumph over me was puerilely obvious, but it put him into a good temper with me, and though I was pretty miserable over losing Antonia I had never really hoped or expected anything else to happen. Pariah dogs, as Antonia herself said succinctly, can't be fussy about their mating.

She said that to me on the only occasion upon which I made any real protest against the marriage. She went on to say that I was selfish to grudge her the measure of security for which she had hoped and waited so long. But before I could assure her that I grudged her nothing, a sly, mischievous look replaced her slightly offended one and she said in quite a different voice, 'Why, Dickon! I've an idea for you, too. Why don't you marry Eloise?'

'Who's she?' I asked gruffly.

'My cousin, Eloise Everard. She lives in Birmingham. She's filthily affluent, quite beautiful—supposed to be my spitting image—and I don't think she's ever had a young man in her life. If you do your stuff properly it should be like taking a baby's bottle.'

'Don't be absurd,' I said. 'There are no young ladies

34

filthily affluent and quite beautiful who are not *besieged* with young men.'

'There are many wonders in the city of Birmingham which you wot not of, young man. Eloise is there, anyway, and she was affluent, beautiful and unattached when I saw her last. And that was, let me see, last autumn, after I'd had 'flu. I was quite glad to crawl there and have a rest. She's got an old Nanny there who is a dragon, but she's a damned good nurse.' 1800372

'I never knew you had a cousin. I wonder you don't grapple her to your soul with hoops of steel—since she's rich, I mean.'

'Again you betray your ignorance of Birmingham. At The Laurels, Merivale Avenue, Birmingham, your body may live in comfort, but the rest of you goes to seed. Breakfast. A little shopping or a visit to the Library. Luncheon. A little rest or a drive, thirty miles an hour, never more. Tea. A quiet read or little amateur gardening. Dinner. Probably a couple of old fogeys in and some bridge at a penny a hundred. My dear, a fortnight of it drives me batty. Eloise has suggested it once or twice, but I just can't cope. I think I would rather beg my bread. At least there'd be the paltry excitement of wondering whether you were going to be given a piece or not.'

'Well,' I said, coming back to the point from which the digression had started, 'you know all about yours now, don't you? Very daintily cut and buttered on both sides.'

'And I'm as good as offering you a similar slice, amn't I? I shall insist upon Eloise coming to the wedding and the rest will be up to you, my handsome young man.'

'It's very heartless of you, Antonia, knowing as you do how I feel about you.'

'I feel the same way about you, idiot. But I haven't let my feelings condemn me to penury or celibacy, have I? Why should you?'

35

'Why indeed?' I could see that there was no purpose to be served by appealing to Antonia, or arguing with her. I let the matter drop and carried on the conversation on the note that she herself had set. 'Tell me more about this phœnix amongst women.'

'Well, there's not much to tell. My mother and Eloise's were twins, a pretty pair, always dressed alike and running in couples—you know the sort of thing. Grandpa had made a little cash out of the bicycle boom or something of the sort and was ambitious for his pretty little daughters. My mother married well, to his great delight. My Poppa's brother was Sir Charles Dimrod, curse his mean black soul, wherever it is. Eloise's mother married one of her father's clerks, in the face of a good deal of opposition, but he was a Very Worthy Young Man, the sort they used to breed, and he had brains. He made a nice pile. I liked Uncle Everard. He paid for my schooling and gave Eloise and me really good holidays. Of course he might have left me a dime but it probably didn't occur to him. My people, you see, after having a heavenly time, all quarrels and reconciliations and Other Women for Poppa and Other Men for Momma and plenty of horse-racing and gambling and a good-time-was-had-by-all for both of them, went down on the *Claratania* when I was ten and left me to charity. Sir Charles never even noticed my existence.'

'And you say Eloise is like you?' It really sounded too good to be true; Antonia, with money to boot.

'In a way, yes. We were always taken for sisters in the old days. Now of course there is more difference. She's kept her hair and she doesn't make up', at least not so that you'd notice. Actually, of course, she's quite different, very shy and retiring and nervous and a bit queer altogether, as you may judge from what I've told you of the way she lives.'

'Not fits or insanity?' I asked. 'Even I draw the line there.'

'Oh no. There's nothing wrong with her that a loving husband couldn't cure. Aunt Ella, you see, lost a baby, a boy that she'd hankered for for years, and went nutty. She put herself out, bang under Eloise's eyes; damned inconsiderate, I always thought, and it shook up Eloise's nervous system. And then there's that damned Nanny, always on the rampage with smelling-salts and hot-water bottles. She makes the whole thing ten times worse, you know, urging Miss Eloise not to over-exert herself, not to get excited, please to drink her nice milk. Completely sickening. Still, you could stop all that, you know, Dickon. And it would be a good thing because then we'd be related in a way and we'd often get chances of meeting that we otherwise wouldn't. I should love my cousin Eloise very dearly indeed if she were Mrs. Richard Curwen.'

'Which just shows what a cold-hearted, unnatural little baggage you are.'

'I'm what the world has made me,' said Antonia comfortably. 'You may find it hard to believe but I was very sentimental as a child, all inky and amorous. Being left to charity cured that, and always seeing Eloise with everything and an adoring father didn't do my ego a lot of good, either. Still, I bear her no grudge. I'm match-making for her. No loving mother could do more.' She laughed.

'Well, the first step in match-making is to produce your filly and trot her around. I'll wait till I've seen her,' I said, and dropped the subject.

Mrs. Campbell extended her hospitality to Eloise, and I happened to be at her house on the day before the wedding when Eloise arrived. I had been sent down with a load of flowers to grace the table for the party which Mrs. Campbell was giving for the bride. Antonia had strolled to the door with me and we stood there talking, when an enormous Rolls, of a superannuated model, purred to a standstill on the gravel. A very old man, roughly disguised as a chauffeur, alighted and opened the door as Antonia and I went forward. Antonia stuck her head in and kissed her cousin and then, still holding her by the hand, dragged her out and made the introduction which was to mean so much.

The newcomer was exactly as Antonia might have been after a long and lowering illness, paler, slighter, less vital, quiet-voiced. She was richly, even beautifully, dressed in a black cloth coat and skirt, the coat lavishly trimmed with silver fox; her hat was fashionable and her shoes elegant, but her appearance as a whole had about as much claim to style as last year's slang. Her hair, the same beech-leaf colour as Antonia's, was dressed in a heavy, lumpish knot at the back of her head, so that her slender neck seemed to droop under the weight of it. Most noticeably of all she lacked entirely her cousin's intriguing suggestion of viciousness. Pale sherry, I decided, compared with Bisquit du Bouché.

But the furs, of course, had cost as much as Antonia had earned in a year and the pearls twisted in a rope round that drooping neck told their own story. Antonia had not lied when she called her cousin affluent. And as she looked at me with wide grey eyes, so like and yet so unlike Antonia's, and gave me a shy little smile, I began to think that there was something in Antonia's suggestion, after all. If I played my cards craftily I might have done with odd jobs like cataloguing libraries, carting dumb youths round the sights of Europe and helping moribund warriors to compose their loathsome memoirs.

Antonia, bless her heart, hard though it was, struck the right note at once. 'Mr. Curwen is arranging the library at Leet for Joshua. He's been very kind to me. Do you remember, Richard, when Dredger was so surly and you ticked him off for me?'

Dredger was Joshua's butler and he feared Antonia as people used to fear the plague. He'd never dreamed of earning a ticking-off on her behalf. But I caught the idea without the eloquent eye-play which Antonia directed at me. Eloise was evidently one of those women—a breed rapidly dying out, and why not?—who liked to see in the male protector a buffer against the world.

'Well,' said Antonia, 'we'll go and find Mrs. Campbell and get your things into your room. Good-bye, Richard, thank you so much for all your help. We'll see you to-morrow.'

'Good-bye, Mr. Curwen,' said Eloise with another shy little smile, and then, 'Why, Parkes, whatever is the matter?'

As I walked away I heard the old man answer, ' 'Tis that brasted lumbago agin. Driving so far at this time a year. 'Tain't fit for yuman beings.'

Not being disposed to show helpfulness by attempting to cope with the lumbago-stricken Parkes, I hastened my stride.

Next day was fine and lovely, one of those golden September days that are as exhilarating and far more subtle than those of early spring with which they have a certain affinity. I suppose ninety per cent of the guests managed to inform Antonia that 'lucky is the bride whom the sun shines on.' And she did look lucky and happy and radiant and beautiful: so beautiful that I felt a pang every time I looked at her. And my feelings towards my employer, paunchy, red-faced old brute, able to marry her just because he had made a packet with his filthy stockbroking, would not have borne examination.

Conscious, however, that I was the best-looking man present and that my clothes were almost the only ones that

39

made any pretence at fitting their owner, I sidled my way into Eloise's company every now and then and saw to it that her glass was replenished and her cigarette lighted at the proper time. I was a little surprised to find that she smoked.

I made little headway. She answered when spoken to and smiled when a smile was needed, but she hardly volunteered a single statement. She looked quite beautiful, too, in a gown of pinkish lace and a wide hat with an ostrich feather, a little darker in shade, laid round it.

Antonia and Joshua drove off in a cloud of rose-leaves and good wishes. Eloise said good-bye to me, as sweetly and vaguely as ever, and drifted away in Mrs. Campbell's wake. And that, I thought, was that. Fortune favoured me, however. Parkes, the old man who drove the Rolls, proved to be really a prey to lumbago. The journey from Birmingham was too much for him, and that evening he was stricken and totally unfit to drive back again on the day after the wedding. Mrs. Campbell rang me up in great distress. 'You see,' she said, 'I mean to shut the house tomorrow, I'm going to Newmarket for the races. I don't want to seem inhospitable to Antonia's cousin but it's very inconvenient for me. She can't travel by train, she gets train-sickness very badly. Can you, Mr. Curwen, think of anyone who could drive her back?'

I pondered for a moment or so and then made two quite impossible suggestions. Mrs. Campbell dismissed them both and then said rather tentatively, 'I was wondering . . .'

'Whether I would,' I said with the kind of frankness that I adopt towards some people. 'I might. In fact I should enjoy doing it. But I'm supposed to be in charge here while my good master is away. Do you think he would mind my absenting myself for a couple of days?'

'I'm sure he wouldn't,' she cooed. 'If anything is said I'll take the responsibility. After all, Miss Everard is Antonia's cousin.'

'Very well,' I said. 'What time would she wish to start?'

40

'You'd better talk that over with her, hadn't you? I'll send her to speak with you. And thank you so much, Mr. Curwen. You've taken a great burden off my mind.'

I waited for a few seconds and then Eloise's shy voice sounded in my ear. 'Mrs. Campbell says that you have offered to drive me home. Are you sure it's convenient?'

'It's decidedly the reverse,' I said. 'But I never have put business before pleasure and this is certainly not the time to begin.'

'What do you mean?'

Oh, God, I thought. Stupid as well. This is going to be an uphill job.

'I mean,' I said clearly, 'that though it may mean sitting up for two whole nights to make up the time, I intend, and nothing shall deter me, to drive you wherever and whenever you wish to go. *Where* is Birmingham, isn't it? And now you tell me *when.*'

'Would ten o'clock be too early?'

'No hour would be too early.'

'I'm sorry to be such a nuisance.'

'But you're not.' I thought of adding, 'You're a lady in distress,' but I decided that that might be too obvious, even for her. So I repeated the hour and said good-bye.

Next morning, carefully and colourfully clad, I presented myself punctually, received some more thanks from Mrs. Campbell, whose car was already waiting, mounted the driver's seat in the Rolls and trundled away. I reckoned Birmingham to be about two hundred and fifty miles away and gathered that I should be able to make good progress in quite another direction in the time that the journey would take. I had forgotten that the driver was separated from the passenger by a thick sheet of glass. That was the first snag; the second, which I soon discovered, was that the car was a devil. There was something wrong with the steering that

41

should have been attended to long before and I could understand why the old fellow had the lumbago. Also, the most it would make was forty miles an hour, all out. It didn't knock or rebel, it slid along smoothly in the best Rolls manner, but after it touched forty it simply ignored the accelerator.

Soon after twelve I decided that something must be done. I kept a sharp look-out for a likely hostelry and presently one appeared. I drew up, got out and opened the door at the back.

'How about a drink?' I asked.

'Oh yes,' she said, smiling. 'Please do.' But she just sat there.

'You'll come, won't you?'

'Oh, shall I?' she asked, and began collecting her bag and her gloves in a flurry. She managed to drop one on the step and was all confusion and gratitude when I handed it back to her.

At first she didn't want to drink anything, then she didn't know what to drink. I ordered her a White Lady and gave careful and rather elaborate instructions as to its mixing. She thought that was a lovely name for a drink and thanked me a lot more for taking so much trouble.

I thought that if I had to sit alone all the way to Birmingham and we didn't get there until about seven o'clock I'd got to start making headway right away. So I adopted some cave-man tactics, blatant and rather rough-edged, but, as it seemed, effective.

I cut short the thanks and said, 'Look here, is this a pose?'

She'd got nice eyes, the same grey as Antonia's, the same eyes, almost, with all the experience and devilry wiped out of them, and now she opened them very wide and fixed them on mine as she said:

'Is what a pose? I'm afraid I don't understand.'

'All this gratitude,' I said brusquely. 'Surely you must

42

know that nobody should be thanked for any trouble he takes to please you. You must know that just to look at you would be . . . well, ample reward for, shall we say, driving that god-awful wagon of yours.'

She ignored the point. 'Is it as awful as all that?' she asked. 'I know it's terribly old. Father bought it, and he's been dead eight years. I've often thought of changing it, but Parkes—he's my man—doesn't seem in favour of it.'

'So you let him bully you, too, do you?'

'Well, I wouldn't say bully. But he gets upset, and I do hate upsetting people.'

'That's the best thing I've heard in an age,' I said. 'So you keep your car to please your man. Parkes is lucky. Have you any other aged retainers who mustn't be upset?'

'No. There's Nanny, of course, but she never upsets me. She's the only one. And she deals with most of the others.'

I got up and rang the bell and repeated the order.

She expostulated when her second drink arrived.

'Go on, you must,' I insisted. 'You should consider the feelings of the poor White Ladies. They get poured down the necks of fat purple women and thin yellow shrews; when one does get the chance to be consumed by somebody fit for a White Lady it must rejoice exceedingly.'

Once again she eluded the obvious compliment.

'I don't suppose they can help being purple or yellow,' she said.

But I was not deterred.

'They're purple because they get more than their share out of life and yellow because they get less,' I said. 'If you're not careful you'll end up yellow.'

That did reach her.

'Why?'

'Well,' I said, 'I don't know you very well, of course. But you're beautiful enough not to feel grateful every time anybody does anything for you; you're rich enough to buy a new car but you don't because of Parkes. I don't call that getting the most out of life. And I dare say if I knew you better I could multiply the examples by a hundred.'

'I dare say you could. But I can't believe that because one has a smooth epidermis and a well-filled purse one should be ungracious and inconsiderate.'

'No,' I said. 'And God forbid that I should suggest it. Life would be a great deal easier for folk like me if there were more like you about.'

'Oh. Would it? Why?'

'Now,' I thought, 'we are getting somewhere.' I started to describe some of the bitches and boors that I had worked for. (I said *worked* because there isn't a word to describe exactly what I do.) I rose to resume the journey in the middle of quite a good story and wondered whether she would bite. She did. After I got the door open for her she paused and said:

'But I can't hear the end of the story if I sit here. Do you mind if I sit with you? It'd be so much jollier.'

So she climbed up beside me and we went bowling along like a naughty chauffeur giving the girl friend a ride.

After that the day was mine. We talked and we talked. I got a pretty good idea of what her life was like. Intensely sheltered, she was like a Sleeping Princess who was too shy even to dream of an awakening. She loved gardening, she told me, and would like to take a house in the country, but had never been able to face the upheaval of a move. She read a great deal, exchanged dinners with a few old friends of her father's, did bits of embroidery, let Parkes take her on drives and went to the theatre fairly often. It sounded a dull programme. In return I told her bits of the story of my life, carefully edited.

All went merry as the proverbial wedding bell until we were on the very outskirts of Birmingham. We'd stopped for lunch and lingered over it a bit and made another halt

44

for tea. It was getting dusk by this time and all along the road, lined with new houses, the lights were springing up in unshuttered rooms. People were beginning to take their dogs out too. One gate opened and out shambled a small man bent on such an errand. The dog that came with him was wildly excited, leaping all over the place and barking. I didn't quite see what happened, but as we drew level a long low car, a beauty, passed us and the dog was by that time off the pavement and was knocked for six. The barking gave way to the most ear-shattering howling. The low car slithered to a standstill and I pulled out to pass it, before I realised what had happened to my passenger. She was slumped down in her seat, half leaning against the door on her side in a species of faint or fit or something.

I stopped the car, shook her shoulder and called her name. Getting no response, I drew upon my memory and I dredged up some forgotten piece of strategy about pushing the head between the knees. I did that, but it didn't work and for one fearful moment I thought that she might be dead.

A fine situation to find oneself in. I got out of the car and accosted the first passer-by, who was, of course, 'a stranger here myself'; but the second person I tackled knew the district and told me that there was a doctor's house straight along the road on the third turning from the left. I drove on there, found the house and pulled the bell. The doctor was out, a woman had called only just ten minutes before and he had gone at once though he'd not had a moment to himself since seven that morning and . . . I cut the story short without ceremony and demanded smelling-salts and brandy. The woman who had answered the door, a housekeeper by the look of her, was evidently used to emergencies. She became very helpful and produced sal volatile as well.

Within about half an hour Eloise was able to continue

the journey. 'You may lean against me if you like,' I said, 'I'm softer than the door.'

She was full of mixed expressions of gratitude and apology to me and of pity for the poor dog. I managed to refrain from saying that there were plenty of dogs in the world and that one less didn't materially affect the scheme of things.

Very soon we arrived in Merivale Avenue, a long wide street planted with plane trees along the pavements and bearing every mark of having been the Mecca of retired Birmingham businessmen between about nineteen hundred and the outbreak of the war. The houses stood in their own grounds, were soundly and squarely built of red brick and had rather pretentious little drives as well as tradesmen's entrances.

'It's the one just past the street lamp on this side,' said my passenger.

The gate was open and I drove in between the laurel and privet bushes and came to a stop before a red brick porch from whose roof hung a lantern.

Before we had alighted the door was torn open and the light from the lantern fell upon a woman of indeterminate age who wore a large white apron over a black silk gown.

'Miss Eloise!' she exclaimed. 'Ah, but I'm glad to see you back. We were beginning to get worried.'

Then she saw me. 'Why, whatever has happened to Parkes?'

'Lumbago,' said Eloise. 'Mr. Curwen kindly drove me home. Have Grey bring in my things, will you, and get the spare room ready.'

By this time we were in the hall and I remember looking round and thinking that it was all so typical that it looked deliberate. It might have been a stage setting for one of those plays which begin in about nineteen hundred and four

46

and go on to show you the family rebelling against Papa, and Mama weeping steadily and the black sheep turning up trumps after all.

The floor was of marble, white and black in squares, and a Turkey carpet ran across it and went on up the stairs, which twisted up to a landing from which another lantern hung. There was a white marble-topped table at the side with a potted fern and a card salver on it. Two antlered heads and a clock decorated the walls, which were covered with faded red paper, and away at the back, under the stairs, there was a stand for sticks and umbrellas and some pegs for coats and hats.

Eloise crossed the hall and opened the door on the left and I finished my inspection with another glance at the white-aproned figure who had welcomed us in. She was looking at me with a glance in which suspicion and distrust were mingled. I knew from that moment that she hated me.

I did not return on the next day, as I had intended.

Eloise, restored to placidity by retiring to bed at nine o'clock and rising at eleven, suddenly changed our relationship by becoming the pursuer, instead of the pursued. Her first ruse was to prolong my stay by asking me to go with her to choose a new car. Her next was to suggest a run out to the city to try out the one we had selected. So it was too late for me to return that day.

We took our meals together in a hideous beetroot-coloured dining room packed with mahogany and silver, and moved on for coffee into a drawing-room in which everything seemed to be abominably frail and pale mauve.

I hated the house. To be in it for an hour cast me into the most hopeless depression. It had such an air of belonging definitely to one time, some past moment when it was the

47

last word of fashion and elegance, that it was like visiting another world, a dead one. I swear that even the air there was vitiated.

I was quite rude about it. Eloise took no offence at all. She merely said that it was exactly as her father had left it and that she had never had the heart to make any changes.

More than once I wondered and was almost prepared to beat a hasty retreat. 'Obviously,' I thought, 'the girl is mental, undeveloped and unbalanced to the point of insanity.' And when I thought of spending every day and every night in such company I told myself that I was also mentally afflicted even to consider such a prospect.

And yet . . . and yet . . . there was quite a lot of sport to be had in going, for instance, into that car depot and being given free choice, in savouring the delightful servility with which we were treated. There was something, too, in being the guest of honour whose tastes were considered in every way and for whom the cellar was ransacked. And, I must admit it, there was a good deal to be said for Eloise's manner towards me, still shy, but venturing timidly upon little intimacies of speech and touch, nervous, placating and adoring.

A young woman may occasionally amuse herself with a man whom she knows to be poor, she may even marry him, but if she is very rich herself and possessed of normal female instincts she takes no trouble to placate him; on the contrary she demands more than the usual amount of service from him and does not hesitate to expose that whip hand, full of lucre. To get a wife who was both rich *and* adoring was not to be sniffed at.

And there was as well the link with Antonia to be considered. And the hope that something might even be made of Eloise. And her undoubted beauty, so like her cousin's.

Taking it all round, I decided that I was pretty fortunate. Before I returned to Meekin's mouldy library I had made

48

up my mind to go right ahead without any more brain harrowing. 'But,' I stipulated to myself, 'we shall leave Birmingham, get rid of every stick in this house and sack every one of these old servants, especially, first and foremost, that acidulated female known as Nanny.'

On the morning before I left, Eloise came down to breakfast. Immediately after she said, 'There's just one more thing I wish you would do for me. Something else to choose that I don't really know much about.'

'Maybe I don't either,' I said. 'What is it?'

'A cigarette case. It's for a man, you see, and men are so funny about things, I always think. I've given presents before which were complete flops.'

My mind immediately ran in two, quite different, directions. One path led me to the conclusion that I was shortly going to receive a gift at her hands. The other track took me to the suspicion that perhaps Eloise was not so simple or so completely unattached as Antonia had led me to believe. After all, was it likely that I should be the only impecunious and not over-scrupulous man in the world? Reason said no. And it occurred to me that Eloise might have a lover tucked away somewhere, maybe abroad, and that she had given him presents that had been flops, probably because they weren't as valuable as he would have liked. It was just possible that I had been bargaining for something that was not in the market at all.

The thought kept me wary as we made our way into the shopping centre and entered the shop that she indicated. It was a good jeweller's, with hardly any evidence of provincialism about it. Here again Miss Everard was recognised and fawned upon, and a selection of gold cigarette cases, ranging in price from thirty to ninety pounds, was laid out for our inspection. Eloise's placid manner gave me no indication that I was to be the lucky recipient, there was no coyness or sidelong looking. I wished there had been, for I was torn two ways. If it were to be mine I could have chosen in an instant—not the most obviously costly, but the best of its kind and size in a medium range. On the other hand, I didn't want to encourage her to spend a large sum on some dim unknown lout.

I handled one or two, enjoying the smooth efficiency of their hinges and snaps, and eventually said, 'I don't think you'll beat that.' The price was forty-seven pounds ten. Eloise took a folded paper from her bag, laid it on the case, handed them both to the man in charge, said, 'As soon as possible, please,' and turned to leave the shop.

So it was for some lout.

I caught the train just before twelve o'clock. Eloise had insisted upon buying me a first-class ticket and just as the train started she put down on the seat beside me a half-pound box of my favourite cigarettes. They cost fifteen shillings but I was not consoled. Also, nothing had been said about any future meeting. I returned to my cataloguing in a depressed frame of mind.

Next morning, however, a registered package for me with a Birmingham postmark sent my spirits soaring. Inside it was the case and inside the case was engraved, 'R.C. With Gratitude. E.E.' and the date.

I sat down to write a very subtle screed in which a nice degree of gratitude, protest that so small a service should be so over-rewarded, and hopes of a meeting in the near future were nimbly mingled. She replied by asking me to spend a week-end as soon as it suited me.

And after that Antonia returned, blooming and beautiful in her new-found security, and just before the work on her husband's library was finished she insisted that her dear cousin Eloise should come to stay. By this time I had flung away all doubts and hesitations. On the third day of her visit I told her that penury, which all my life had thwarted me, had now wrecked my heart and my hopes. Ten minutes were wasted in explaining and elaborating this statement and fifteen minutes later we were engaged.

I was surprised to find that Eloise was just as anxious to sell the Birmingham house and break all the links of her old life as I was for her to do it. Only upon one thing was she firm. Nanny must come with us. She explained to me that Nanny, then a buxom girl of twenty, had been with her at the crisis of her life, had supported and comforted her then and ever since, understood her as no one else could ever do and was quite indispensable.

I argued the point for a long time. I explained that I was now proposing to be to her what the woman had been, and that it would be better to make a completely clean break with everything that had belonged to the past. In vain. Upon this one question Eloise showed all the stubbornness of the weak, and when she began to cry and turn pale and shiver I had no choice but to give in. I could not say that the sight of Emma Plume was distasteful to me, or that I hated the woman because she had once looked at me with eyes which saw clean through all my intentions, all my hopes and all my schemes.

So I said, 'Very well, darling. She shall come,' and went on to talk about something else.

Antonia and I had managed to find time for a private talk and had decided that for Eloise and me to take a place somewhere a few miles away was the best thing to do. It would be easier than carrying on an intrigue in a village where we both lived. So although there were two houses to sell within ten minutes' walk of the Meekins' place Eloise and I ignored them and went farther afield. And we found the ideal house in a village called Copham.

It was called the Chimney House because it had high,

beautifully twisted Elizabethan chimneys that showed up amongst the trees. It was not over-large and unless I had known that Eloise had plenty of money to spend on it I should not have looked at it twice. For nothing is more uncomfortable than a country house without proper sanitation, lighting or water.

But we had the money and Eloise was willing to spend it. Bathrooms were made in queer little bedrooms, the thick beams were drilled and electric wires laid. A surprisingly efficient gardener was discovered and the garden almost relaid. It grew into as snug and pretty a little property as one could wish.

Throughout the whole time of our engagement Eloise was as happy and elated as a child on its birthday. Her delight over the buying and reconstruction of the house amazed me. Once I said to her, "Did it never occur to you that you could perfectly well have done this years ago?' And she replied, as she always did to any suggestion of making an effort on her own initiative, with a little shrinking movement.

'Oh, but I couldn't. I couldn't have faced it all by myself. With you it is heavenly.'

We had a piece of luck over the Merivale Avenue house. It proved to me what I have always suspected, that to those who have shall always be given—in the financial line. The district was out of favour, it was smart to live farther out these days, and the house itself was old-fashioned. So we had decided that if it made a thousand pounds we should be well content. But it so happened that within five minutes' walk of Merivale Avenue the Council had built a colony of new houses in connection with the slum-clearance scheme, and this, which might have taken hundreds of pounds off the value of the house, on the contrary put hundreds on. For the Council, ever anxious in the cause of its citizens, desired a house in the vicinity to be turned into a public library and recreation centre. They paid four thousand for the place without blinking. They even bought the great dining-table for one of the public rooms.

I saw to the selling of it. Eloise said that she never wanted to see Birmingham again and was far too happy looking after Chimney House to bother about what happened in Merivale Avenue. She seemed to think that the inflated price had been obtained through my cleverness and when it was definitely settled she gave me a great and very pleasant surprise. She insisted upon transferring the four thousand pounds, plus the twenty for the table, into my account. I admit that it was far more money than I had— before meeting her—ever dreamed or hoped of possessing.

Still, I told myself, all the favours were not on one side. If I gave her nothing else I did give her a zest for living. I taught her how to spend. I was always on tap, as it were, for the supply of advice, sympathy and confidence. She was helpless, defenceless and inexperienced as a child: if the slightest thing went wrong she despaired, collapsed, wept and literally wrung her hands. I considered that I had earned the four thousand by the time that I had the house fit to live in, the furniture chosen, the curtains hung and the staff engaged.

We were married just before Christmas and went to Capri for our honeymoon. It was delightful for me to travel again, and to be travelling without keeping an eye either upon the expenses or upon some half-baked youth who was in my charge, which was how my former trips had been made. It was pleasant, too, to be able to impress Eloise with my knowledge of languages and exchanges and my ability to obtain attention and service and my capacity for finding out when and whence trains started. That honeymoon trip showed exactly how desirable was a partnership like ours;

she couldn't have travelled without me, and I couldn't have travelled without her money. We had a wonderful time and Eloise obviously became more attached to me every day.

Still, I was not sorry to return to Copham. Since that day, or rather night, some ten months before, when I had first kissed Antonia, my heaven had been wherever she was and I was eager to get back and discover a workable plan for our future meetings. In some obscure way the pseudo-affection and simulated passion which I was compelled to show to Eloise sharpened my yearning for the one real and valid connection that I had ever made. And there was no hope of what the psychologists call 'transference,' that is, in thinking that Eloise was Antonia. They might have similar features and the same kind of hair. Their method of loving was as different as their method of living.

Once or twice it did shoot through me that Antonia with her squat elderly husband and I with my faery child wife had in reality sold our birthright for a mess of pottage. After all, it is few people who ever do meet their perfect person as Antonia and I had done in one another, and it is an experience not lightly to be despised. However there was nothing to be gained by thinking that way. Antonia and I had had our cake, we were both in the money, now we must see if there wasn't some way of regaining some cake and getting at least part of the birthright back. I hurried home to the Chimney House, Copham, as to the anteroom of paradise.

And for a time it did seem that Antonia and I were favourites of the gods, bound by no mortal law. Joshua Meekin, her husband and my ex-employer, had retired from the Stock Exchange with wads of money and big ideas. He had tried to turn Leet Hall into a country seat and it was to aid him with his entertaining that Antonia had been imported, just as I had been brought in to settle his library.

54

The fact that he had married his housekeeper—so fatal an act to many social aspirants—was more than compensated by the fact that Antonia was of 'good family.' 'Her uncle was tenth baronet and her father would have had the title but he was drowned at the sinking of the *Claratania*, you know.' They overlooked the small matter of the tenth baronet having completely washed his hands of his niece and abandoned her to a pariah existence like an alley cat; and of her father having been a spendthrift rascal. The County were quite unable to resist Antonia's claims to recognition now that they were backed by Joshua's money, generosity and good nature. Joshua was soon hunting twice a week and either giving or attending shooting parties regularly.

Antonia, who neither shot nor hunted, became an indefatigable payer of calls. She had her own car, a cream-coloured Lagonda, and it shot about the countryside carrying Antonia on her many visits. Ten minutes or a quarter of an hour looking at gardens or babies or spent in local gossip was enough to establish an alibi, and then she would rush to some place previously appointed where I was waiting, and the rest of the afternoon was heaven.

And I? I was free because soon after our return from Capri, Eloise discovered that she was to have a baby. Immediately Emma Plume became the governor of her days. As the Psalmist says of the Lord, she governed her uprising and her downsitting, and one of her rules was that every afternoon Miss Eloise, as she called her, must completely undress and get, as she expressed it, 'between the sheets.'

I had no fault to find with this dictum. For one thing, it left me freer than I had hoped to be. For another, I do believe that the regime suited Eloise. Certainly she was more stable and healthy during this period than she had ever been before or was to be again.

About ten miles to the east of Copham there was a stretch

of that peculiar country known, I believe, as Breckland. It was a wild and uninhabited region, all pine trees, Scots firs, gorse and scrubby turf. Some years before, soon after the war, there had been an attempt to make a settlement of unemployed there, to breed pigs and chickens. The men, brought from warm swarming warrens of the slums, had either decamped, rebelled, or gone melancholy mad and the attempt had been abandoned. A few mouldering huts and a few yards of wire-netting were all that remained of the government's misguided philanthropy. Here, on the grass and bracken between the gorse bushes on good days, or in the shelter of a tumble-down hut in bad ones, Antonia and I met and enjoyed our birthright. It sounds risky, but really it was not so. The place was as lonely as one would find in the British Isles. We left our cars on the by-road where no one came, and in separate places at that; we pushed through prickly gorse and brambles which no one would have faced unless they were bent upon a similar errand to our own or were definitely out to spy; and we were publicly the soul of discretion.

For we met publicly, of course, in our own houses and in other people's. Hundreds of times have I looked across a lighted dinner-table and seen Antonia, laughing and indulging in her particular brand of light flirtation, and thought, 'Yes, my beauty. Five hours ago you were all my own.'

It was like having a secret treasure laid away. It sent me back restored and strengthened, able to make the effort to amuse and cherish Eloise, to face Emma Plume's scornful scrutiny, to bear the little pin-pricks of discomfort and embarrassment that must always beset a poor man who has married his wife for her money.

Oh yes, Antonia and I had each married for money and kept our love as well.

In that winter there were dances too. Public ones in aid of local charities and private ones given at big houses.

Eloise, early on, attended them, looking frail and lovely, dancing only a few times and never at a loss for someone to sit out with. Old gentlemen loved her, and she, in her newly found security and confidence, could say her little set speeches and smile her sweet little smile as they danced attendance on her. Joshua, who did not care for dancing, used to pump-handle Antonia twice or thrice round the floor and then give her to more active partners, while he stood by, looking on like an amiable penguin. We always managed several dances together, and more often than not were able to steal away somewhere for an embrace, as passionate as it was momentary, though we were very careful. Very careful indeed.

It was a good time. But, of course, like all good times, it ended. Eloise gave birth to our daughter at the end of October. She was exceedingly ill and the baby was a wailing, ailing little thing. Emma Plume came into her own again, and it no longer seemed foolish to address her as Nanny.

When Eloise was about again I became conscious of a change in her. It was as though the normal process of motherhood had compensated for those frustrated and stultifying years. She delighted to do things for the child, took a great interest in the running of the nursery, and through these channels seemed to find herself. She was more confident, too, and far, far more demanding. Affectionate as ever and docile over many things still, she was nevertheless far removed from being a faery child wife and I was soon made to feel the difference. I began to long for a job. I wished that I had an office, where I could be 'delayed.' I was not fitted for country life. No sport has ever held even a passing attraction for me. I had chosen to live at Copham because of Antonia; if barriers were now to be raised between us my life would be empty indeed.

57

And there was a barrier. Eloise. What chance now had I of stealing away to the camp in the afternoon? Eloise liked to be driven. She must come. Just occasionally she went out calling, and then Ted, the gardener and occasional chauffeur, might be allowed to drive her (she much preferred me to) and then perhaps I might telephone to Antonia and she would rush over to see 'dear Eloise and the baby,' find Eloise out, appease Nanny by admiration of the baby and so snatch an hour or so with me. But it was uncertain and risky and could not be allowed to happen too often.

That winter, too, Joshua was smitten with asthma and Antonia had to accompany him upon a cruise. We could have gone, too, easily enough—Nanny was more than capable of looking after the baby—but of course Eloise would not hear of it. That warm airy nursery had been made for Diana and there Diana was to be. And where Diana was, Eloise would be, and there should I be also.

And I had no alibi. I earned my bread by being Eloise's husband and Diana's father, and if it happened to be a whole-time job what right had I to complain?

It began to dawn upon me that perhaps Antonia and I had been, not the favourites of the gods, but their sport. We had been given a taste of what we might have had and were now to be left with what we had chosen.

Jealousy nagged at me too. Part of Antonia's attraction for me lay in my never being absolutely sure of her. I did not flatter myself that she would remain faithful to my memory if she found herself on board a boat with an attractive man in tow. Joshua's good nature and asthma and his passion for playing cards made him an unreliable chaperon. Oh hell! What I endured that winter!

I made a definite attempt at one juncture to get the malady out of my blood. There's nothing else on earth that I really care about—except my own comfort: my nature is cold and calculating, my mind reasonable. Why should I be so much at the mercy of one small passion? Why should my happiness be so dependent upon one woman? As well ask the tide why the moon pulls it. There *is* no answer.

They were due to come home in May. I lived for their arrival, and all the time I was an attentive, affectionate, amenable and necessary piece of furniture about the Chimney House.

Antonia rang up on the evening of their arrival and suggested that we should go along to Leet Hall for drinks to celebrate their safe return. It was the hardest job I had ever set myself to walk into that room with Eloise and give Antonia the careful greeting that was demanded. She was all golden tan so that the colour from her russet hair seemed to have run into her flesh. Her hair was done differently, too, and she had used a new brilliant orange lipstick. I ached with longing for her.

Joshua was restored to health, full of spirits and plans; Eloise disposed to talk about the baby; and just once Antonia and I were able to draw a little apart, to stand by the French window, to move a step outside on to the terrace.

'I must speak to you,' I muttered. And she turned and called over her shoulder, 'I'm just taking Richard to see the rockery. You'd better not come, darling, there's quite a nip and after the heat it might get you.'

'God, I've missed you,' I said.

'And I you, Richard.' Her hand was hanging by her skirt; I brushed the back of my own against it and strange fiery thrills ran over me. Nothing, nothing that Eloise could ever do could give me a thousandth part of the thrill which the mere touch of Antonia's fingers sent through me.

'I've got to see you,' I said, staring unseeing at the flaming colours of the rock garden.

59

'I've got an idea. See my hair? It's impossible to get it done like this anywhere but in London. It depends on the cut. At the end of next week I shall run up, just for the day. Can you think up an alibi for just one day, say Thursday or Friday?'

'I must, I will,' I said. 'I suppose we'd better get back now. I'll ring you up if I don't see you and tell you how I'm fixed.'

Since Eloise did not wish to leave the baby for a whole long day I was able to go to London to see about a suit of clothes, unaccompanied. I knew some flats that could be hired for the day, and if the full charge was paid nobody worried whether the temporary tenant was there for twenty-four hours or only for a short time in the afternoon.

That day opened the second phase. It was more pregnant of risk than the other. Joshua and Eloise had only to notice once that their respective mates were invariably absent on the same days for the whole situation to blow sky-high. I had a certain difficulty in finding excuses. There was a limit to the number of suits I could order. So I adopted a conscientious attitude and said that I thought that I ought to find myself some odd jobs in the literary line: I could not be idle all my life. I wrote to one or two people who had been helpful in the past and arranged to lunch with them. They were willing to meet me when they realised that I was now in a position to pay for the luncheons. I seemed to have more friends than I had been aware of in the lean days. I got a little reviewing—boring enough but more than welcome since it gave me an interest outside Copham and a reason for more frequent absences.

The second summer stole by, crammed with as many clandestine meetings as we could contrive. They were rare enough and their rarity kept the appetite unsated, the flame of passion alive. Eloise was always pleased when I returned with some little offering for her or for Diana. In fact, during this period everybody seemed happy and content.

In the following December came the Woodhouse crash. A so-called multi-millionaire blew out his brains in a Paris flat, and as though that shot had been the first fired in a secret war, people began to die by various means all over the world. Spinsters whose slender incomes had disappeared slid a final shilling into the gas meter and lay down beside the oven door. Rich men, suddenly beggared, opened windows in the thirtieth floor of New York apartment houses and hurtled down into the street. Colonels turned their guns on themselves, and meek clergymen tried overdoses of aspirin.

Joshua Meekin was not driven to take his life by any violent means; he read a simple paragraph in his morning paper, turned purple, gasped for breath and fell down in an apoplectic fit on his own hearth. Once again poor Antonia was at the mercy of the world. Her period of security had lasted just two years and a few months. Except that she had a few jewels and a well-stocked wardrobe, she was just where she had been before.

Eloise's money, conservatively invested, was untouched. Antonia, all in black and with a suitable make-up, was an appealing figure. Eloise, grateful for her own unaffected position, needed very little guileful handling to bring her to the point of offering, for the second time, the shelter of her roof to her cousin. And this time Antonia accepted it.

At first we were wildly excited. The prospect of being under the same roof, able to meet openly every day, was delightful and delirious. In practice we discovered that it made everything frightfully difficult. Also, though this may have been the by-product of a guilty conscience, I seemed to be aware of Emma Plume watching us—that is, Antonia

61

and me—with eyes made sharp by hatred and suspicion. I saw her, several times, leaning out of the nursery window, watching us when we set off for a walk or a drive on the few times that we could steal away. She seemed almost to patrol the corridor at night, and was given to throwing open the door of any room that held us two alone for a minute, without warning, and to asking, 'Is the mistress here?' in a way that added, 'She should be!' I mentioned the matter to Antonia, warning her to beware the hag. Antonia said, 'Oh, it's only that she hates me, and loathes my being here. She always has hated me. She used to be terribly unjust to me when I stayed with Eloise in the holidays, years ago.'

We managed just one or two trips to London in the first six months of that year. I suggested that Antonia should come up and see some of the people who had found me jobs, in the hope that they might do as much for her. That gained us one day. Another time she asked me, openly, across the table, whether I would accompany her to see about disposing of some of her jewels. Eloise protested at that and said that she would let her have any money she wanted, but money wasn't the whole of it; Antonia insisted upon going to London.

We did that twice. And it was a warning against pulling any trick a second time. We'd gone up by train because Eloise was going out to tea and wanted the car. And the train suited us in a way: we could give one another undivided attention. In the evening we arrived at Cambridge, where we had to change for the final twenty miles in a slow local train, and found that it had been discontinued.

We might, of course, have hired a car to drive us to Copham, but the idea no sooner occurred to us than we dismissed it. A whole night together was something not to be missed. It might be years before it came our way again. But, my God, we needed to be careful!

We were. We took separate rooms on different floors of a hotel. We used our own names. We were as open as the day. But lovers before me have climbed midnight stairs, have knocked and been admitted.

I had telephoned to Eloise, saying that we had missed the train, but I did not say that we were within twenty miles of home, knowing that she would have sent into the village and routed Ted out of bed and despatched him to fetch us. I pretended, too, that the line was very bad and said that I could hardly hear her, muffling my own voice to give the lie verisimilitude. That would account, I thought, for the shortness and vagueness of my conversation. So I was not prepared to face much of a scene when I arrived home.

Eloise was in bed: Emma Plume was riding her highest horse. Miss Eloise had been very upset last night, she had had one of 'her turns,' all because I had sounded so vague and distant that she was sure something had happened and I had tried to hide it from her. No, I could not go in and speak with her because she had just fallen asleep for the first time since last night. The woman's manner plainly informed me that she, at least, knew her worst suspicions justified. And when Eloise awoke and was permitted, at last, to receive me, I felt that there was something a little queer about her manner too. For one thing, she asked me point-blank where I had stayed, and when I said, 'At Cambridge,' she went on and on about my folly in not asking for Ted to fetch us.

'But he had gone home. It was getting late and it seemed stupid to cause such a commotion. After all, we weren't exactly stranded, or in danger of discomfort.' She looked at me oddly and said, 'No. I don't suppose you minded.' And I realised that she and Nanny had had a heart-to-heart

63

talk in the watches of the night and that the seed of doubt, if not of actual suspicion, had been well and truly sown. Not—I'll give the old cow her due—not that she would take any pleasure in unsettling Eloise's mind, but because she wanted Antonia uprooted before anything might happen which *must* be noticed by Eloise. A kind of precautionary measure.

It all blew over. But it had the effect of making Antonia and me more careful, which amounted to making us keep apart and hankering after the forbidden fruit more than ever. Antonia cracked first. We had taken, in desperation, to a passionate bout of gardening. The garden was large, and although Eloise spent hours in it every day and Ted gave it most of his time, it was quite possible for the four of us to be out of hearing of one another, and if Antonia and I bent over one bed, weeding, or stood on opposite sides of a herbaceous border, tying up heavy plants or snipping off dead flowers, we were apparently harmless enough and at the same time could talk about what we liked.

We were working like that one day when she said, 'I can't stick this any longer, Dick. Seeing you and not being able to snatch even long enough to talk is unadulterated hell. I'm going to get a job again.'

My heart fell away, leaving all my chest hollow. I knew what that meant. Antonia was hungering for the old life; the old, promiscuous rough-and-tumble, the taking of chances and of lovers. If I let her go I should lose her, maybe for ever. I looked across the delphiniums we were staking and tying with blue bass, and took in every line of her loveliness as though I were seeing it for the first, or the last, time. That small head set so proudly on the long slim neck, that cunningly planed and tinted face, the mouth I had kissed so often; the full bosom and the sudden smallness of her waist, the long thighs and slender legs. Then I turned my head and watched Eloise carrying some rubbish to the pile that lay on the edge of the far shrubbery. So alike, with such a deadly difference! There they were, the two people in the world who held, between them, all that I cared for, Eloise with her money, Antonia with her charm. Oh, for some magic that would combine them in one. If only Antonia could keep me, Eloise charm me!

'Don't go,' I said, and was surprised at the urgent humility of my own voice. 'I'll think of something.'

'Thinking won't help,' she retorted. 'You must *do* something.'

Something snapped in my head. I felt the hot wave of it run all over my face; my ears roared and I could hardly see. 'I will,' I said. 'I'll ask Eloise to divorce me. I was fool enough once to let you put money first and to put it first myself. But that's over. I'll get a job and I'll work at it . . . if you'll marry me.'

Antonia laughed, dropped her bass and stooped for it, looking up at me through the flowers like a seductive nymph.

'Don't be such a fool,' she said. 'For one thing, Eloise would never do it. For another, imagine how soon we should hate one another, living on five pounds a week after having what we've had.'

'We'd be together,' I said stubbornly.

'Not long. My sweet Dickon, I think the sun must have gone to your head, I've never heard you babble before.'

'What do you suggest then?'

'That you renounce connubial bliss for a little while and come up and see me sometime.' She swaggered away to the end of the row with a tolerable imitation of Mae West.

Easily said. But not so easily done when a man has a wife who is affectionate and clinging, and who is, moreover, prone to nightmares from which she wakes, trembling and sweating, avid for the comfort of human presence. I dithered upon the brink of making a suggestion for several days, but each time the words stuck in my throat and I felt that my intention would scream aloud through any speech I might use to disguise it. Finally I said, 'You go away, Antonia. Stay away a week or ten days and when you come back I'll have it fixed.'

So Antonia invented, or wangled, an invitation and departed, and as soon as she had gone I took to sleeping badly, waking and stumbling about the room in search of something, or to open the window for more air, and I took care to wake Eloise each time. After three nights of it she was prepared to listen to my plans for sleeping in another room while the hot weather lasted.

Antonia stayed away for three weeks and by the time she returned I was installed in a room near the stairs and the custom was established.

Everything went well until late in September. The weather stayed warm and Eloise said nothing about my return to her. She would do so, of course, in time, and I should return promptly and have to think up something else. And then it happened.

I was up in Antonia's room, which was about half a flight above my own, Eloise's and the nursery. It was about one o'clock in the morning and I was lying, drowsy and satisfied, delaying the imminent moment when I must wrench myself away and return to my own place. Suddenly I heard a kind of muffled thudding on the floor below and knew, with a sudden access of horror, that someone was knocking on my door. I slid on to the floor, pushed my feet into my slippers and wrapped my dressing-gown round me. I went down the stairs in the darkness, but the light was on on the lower floor and there was Emma Plume, her hair in curlers and her face distraught, turning the knob of my door. I ought, of course, to have stolen away upstairs, passed Antonia's door on the half-landing, gained the top floor, descended the servants' stairs and come *up* to the corridor where the woman stood. I could have said that I had been walking on the terrace, I could have said anything. But I thought of it too late. I was not in a state of mind to be resourceful, and before my head took charge of me the nurse turned and saw me, half poised for flight upon that lower stair. And at the same moment Eloise, her hair streaming and her eyes dazed with sleep, opened the door opposite and said, 'Oh, what is the matter?'

'The baby's got croup,' said Emma Plume. 'It's a bad attack, too. We must have the doctor.'

Eloise screamed. I said, 'I'll fetch him, that'll be quickest,' and Emma Plume said something about getting a hot bath and doing the best she could until he came. But all the time there lay, between the three of us, so obviously occupied and engrossed with the baby's croup, the deeper and darker matter of my appearance upon those stairs.

I pushed past Eloise and Emma Plume at the doorway of the nursery and fled to the garage exactly as I was. The doctor had just put his car away, after coming back from a maternity case, and was still dressed and awake. We were back at the Chimney House in record time.

While he dealt with the baby I dressed myself properly, and when the attack subsided I drove him home. I then drove on for quite a distance in the night, trying to settle what should be said to Eloise. It depended, I decided, upon Antonia. By this time I was so infatuated that if she were willing to marry me I should not trouble to defend myself to Eloise.

Breakfast appeared punctually. Eloise did not come down, but while I poured my first cup of coffee Antonia slid into the room looking furtive and disagreeable.

'You mug,' she greeted me. 'Why didn't you bolt to the top floor and down the service stairs? I followed you out and stood there hissing, "Come back," but you never so much as turned your head. Just stood there, the picture of guilt discovered. I could kill you.'

'I thought of that too late,' I said sulkily. 'It's no good going into that now. The question is, what are we going to tell Eloise? I'm willing to tell her to do her worst, if you'll marry me afterwards.'

'You haven't any money and last night proved that you haven't any sense, either,' said Antonia harshly, setting down her cup with a clatter and reaching for a cigarette. 'Whether Eloise divorces you or not is her affair, and yours. But don't think that I'm going to share love in a cottage or a frowsty boarding-house with you. You're all right in bed, if you'll excuse my plain speaking, but out of it you're useless. I think, though I may be nearing the sere and yellow, that I could do better for myself.'

'All right,' I said, 'do it. I'm afraid you're finished here.'

'I know. I've been packing since six.'

The finality of that cut into me. I went round the table and took her by the shoulders. 'You're a devil,' I said, and she laughed, still disagreeably. 'Once more, and for the last time, will you let me come with you and try to make a go of it?'

'No,' she said, shrugging away from me. 'You go and make your peace with the Blessed Damozel. Then you'll maybe be able to slide out to see me from time to time, and occasionally slip me a fiver. As I said, you're excellent in bed.'

Angry as I was, and hurt and affronted, I seized the crumb of comfort that lay in her last words. As a husband, a penniless husband, she had no use for me at all. As a rich woman's husband, still in love with her, I should have my uses. She saw that I was weakening and snatched her opportunity. She leaned up and kissed me once, warmly

68

and closely. Then she said, 'I'll be seeing you,' and went away to finish packing.

So that was that. So much for the only uncalculating offer I had ever made any woman!

Eloise came down soon afterwards.

'The coffee's cold,' I said, and went towards the bell.

'Never mind,' she said, 'I had some tea upstairs with Nanny. Richard, I want to talk to you. Antonia must leave this house and never come back. I won't ask how long this has lasted, nor whose is the fault. When she has gone we will forget all about it. But I should like your word that it won't happen again, either with her or anyone else.'

One woman had treated me scornfully that morning, I was hanged if another was going to hand out the same dose. 'You speak as though I had been caught stealing jam.' I sounded even angrier than I felt. 'Say that you want a divorce. I won't deny that I have given you grounds. But for God's sake don't speak to me like a tolerant mother addressing a naughty boy.'

It was, perhaps, the most openly offensive thing I had ever said to her and it shattered once and for ever the false superficial veneer of friendliness that had lain over our relationship. It struck away the rather childlike dignity with which she had seated herself and spoken to me. I saw her face whiten and her eyes widen as though I had dealt her a physical blow.

'I shall never divorce you, Richard,' she said, 'though I have never thought that you could speak so cruelly to me.'

'Oh,' I retorted impatiently, forgetting that honesty between us was an untried thing and likely to be fatal, 'I'm sorry if I sound cruel: but we might as well look facts in the face. You know now about Antonia and, odd as it may

69

seem, I am not going to apologise about it. That would be silly. You can choose your own course. You can ignore the whole thing, or you can make an issue of it and have your divorce. I don't care much either way.'

I was too raw and smarting to care about tact or anything else. While the affair could be kept secret I was willing to go to some lengths to conceal it, but it was too late now, and when I said that I did not care either way, I spoke neither more nor less than the truth. For the moment the thought that Antonia was leaving, that she was going out into the world where I could not see her easily, nor even know what she was doing, blinded me to all else.

'I believe you want me to divorce you,' said Eloise in an ominous voice.

'I've told you. I'm indifferent. You, as the injured party, have the choice of weapons. Use either without scolding. That is all I ask.'

She stood up suddenly and clutched her hands together.

'All right then, I'll choose, as you call it. I will not divorce you. I'll never divorce you. Partly because of Diana, and partly because I will not hand you over to Antonia. I will not! But neither will I forgive you while you hold to that attitude. Even though I love you, Richard. Even though the knowledge of your infidelity, under my very roof, has upset me more than I can tell you. I never thought, never dreamed . . .' She broke off and into her eyes there came that fixed, dreadful stare. She dropped down again into the chair and put her head on the table, so that Antonia's unemptied cup of coffee spilled across the cloth and her own hair dragged in the marmalade.

'I can't bear it,' she sobbed. 'I can't bear this kind of thing. You've spoiled it all. You've spoiled my life and you don't care a bit. It's too awful, I can't bear it.'

She began to beat the table with her head and the arms of the chair with her hands. It was not a pretty sight. I knew that I ought to have gone to her, taken her in my arms and promised her anything if she would only forgive me and calm herself. But I just couldn't do it. I stood there as though I had been paralysed, and as I looked upon the exhibition of her emotion the only one of which I was conscious was one of intense repulsion. First she had come down like an injured Madonna and addressed me with cold dignity; and now she was behaving like an hysterical child. Ordinary anger, normal resentment I could have met and dealt with, but not this. My only fear was that she would do herself an injury. I went to the foot of the stairs and roared for Nanny. Then I took myself out of the house and did not go back until late at night.

I believe that I began to hate Eloise from that morning.

But it was more than four years before I did anything about it. I will dismiss them quickly, those four tedious years.

For quite a while, at least a fortnight after Antonia's going, Eloise preserved a stony, sulky silence, shutting herself in her room or the nursery, and being tended and comforted by Emma Plume, who all the time looked at me balefully when we met. Several times during that fortnight I was on the verge of saying, 'Look here, Eloise, we can't go on like this. I'm sorry for what's happened and it's over and done with. Do let's think of some working arrangement for the rest of our lives.' If she had been normal I would have said something like that; but dread of the scene that would almost inevitably follow any stirring of old emotion held me silent and so, like all women who find a man obdurate, she made the first move. She had her hair done and came down to dinner one night in a new dress, as expensive and lovely and unstylish as any of her others, and she chatted resolutely and brightly about Diana and the garden and little bits of local gossip and gradually gave me

71

to understand that the affair was to be ignored. I was only too glad to play back to her and so the second stage set in. For more than a month there was nothing that she would not have done to please me. She gave me money, she gave me presents, she listened to every word I said as though pearls were dripping from my lips, she even suggested a trip abroad, but she withdrew that suggestion when she found that I accepted it seriously and decided that she could not leave the baby.

I made what response I could, but it was very little and must have been very unsatisfactory from her point of view. For with Antonia's going something had dried up in me. The spirit and spring had gone so that I couldn't even pretend any longer. I could be polite and attentive and considerate to Eloise and no more.

But she, at least, had interests and outlets for her feelings. She had her garden, the house, Emma Plume and the child. I had nothing! I sometimes seemed to catch a glimpse of myself going through life like a pet animal on a lead. But after all it was what I had chosen, and I would have resigned myself. With almost any other woman in the world, barring an out-and-out shrew, I would have settled down into an amiable jog-trot of existence, grateful at least that my roof was watertight and my meals were certain. With Eloise this was impossible.

Even now, looking back, I find it difficult to say exactly why this was so, or to give any reason for our frequent and virulent quarrels. People as incompatible and far less civilised have lived together for years without anything approaching the number of storms we encountered. But I suppose such people have one solvent, either sexual passion or a common aim in life or merely a mutual war against the world to wage in order to make a living. Without any of these our life became a little hell closed within four walls. Rows began out of nothing, flamed, died down, were followed by reluctant apologies and a few hours of armed truce, and then at the slightest words, even at the inflection of a voice, sprang up again.

Almost every difference of opinion resulted in Eloise falling into one of her fits of frenzy. She would cry, beat her hands and her head, even fall to the floor and drum her heels on the carpet. And with each attack I turned into stone, standing by and watching with a sharp eye and indifferent mind until she lapsed into semi-consciousness. Then I could move and shake off my paralysis, slap her hands (which I did with a good deal of pleasure), thrust ammonia under her nose or dribble brandy between her clenched teeth. All these I did with a distaste that custom could not stale; and I did it often enough, for just at this time Emma Plume was busy with the baby, and although she knew, more than any other living person, the state of affairs between us, she did not know either how frequent or how deadly were our quarrels.

Oddly enough, they were rarely concerned with money, which might have been expected to provide a fruitful field for disagreements. I still had a little left from the price of the Birmingham house which Eloise had given me in the early days of her newly aroused affection; and as long as that lasted I was determined not to ask for more. But soon after Antonia's going Eloise started upon a new phase: from being almost comically parsimonious, considering her income, she began to spend wildly. Fantastic, expensive, unfashionable clothes filled every cupboard of the house. For Diana's benefit an enormous sun-parlour of Vita glass was built at one end of the house, and in the garden, at great expense, a swimming-pool was made with one railed-in end, about a foot deep, so that Diana might get accustomed to the water and from that proceed with confidence to learn to swim, 'as native children do,' said Eloise, who was herself terrified of bathing.

Besides spending as recklessly as she could in her limited way, she gave away a great deal of money. Hardly an appeal came into the house and stayed unanswered. The East End slummers had only just finished needing coal and winter comforts before they must be sent to the sea for the summer. The running expenses of the Chimney House, modest except where Diana was concerned, were outweighed every year by its mistress's contributions to charity. All very nice and noble and I did not begrudge it, until one day when Eloise said:

'Really, Richard, we must begin to save some of our income.' (Good hearing for me who had none!) 'Otherwise if anything happens to me you'll be on the rocks. You see, Father made a peculiar will. The money goes to my legal issue or, failing that, to various social services in Birmingham. You'd have nothing. So we must save.'

I gave her full marks for this kindly and practical thought, but they were prematurely awarded. Almost the very next day she decided that Diana needed sea air in greater quantities and of more assured purity than any seaside resort could offer, so she chartered a yacht for three months and we pottered about the Mediterranean and the Ægean through the summer, and Eloise frowned upon landing trips because all foreign places were hotbeds of infection. I did practically die of boredom. And for the first time I grudged the cost of it all: I had verified her statement about the old man's will and realised that I had only Eloise—or her savings—between me and the cold world again. And then I realised that her remark about saving had been a taunt; one which dumbly repeated itself every time she bought some totally unnecessary object and told me the price of it.

In all this time I preserved some uncertain communication with Antonia. True, she wrote seldom and in four years we managed to meet only three times. But I always

74

knew to within a little what she was doing and with whom she was. She had got into touch with an association known as the Helpers' Club, which specialised in finding odd jobs for women and women for odd jobs. It would provide you, at a moment's notice, with a cook, a secretary, a governess or a nurse; it would have your dog exercised, your flat furnished, your luggage packed, your offspring taken to the dentist. It was a useful and commendable organisation, but I couldn't quite picture Antonia in its ranks. However, through its mediation, she—who was probably younger, better-looking and a cleverer showman than most of its workers—obtained several good jobs. Since most of them were temporary they suited her well, though one casual engagement extended to several months, during which she shepherded across the Atlantic and back again an old lady who wished to visit her daughter in Jamaica but dared not make the journey alone.

She wrote me laconic, amusing letters, making fun both of her own hatred of the jobs and of the jobs themselves. But even as I smiled over them I dreaded turning the page, fearing to come upon the triumphant announcement that in some house, somewhere, she had found another Joshua Meekin. I could not imagine any man seeing her without wanting her and, circulating as she did, she was bound to meet and charm many men.

Most often the letters ended with an appeal for money, which I always sent—out of the house money as long as it lasted, and after that by the simple procedure of forging Eloise's signature upon a cheque. A few hours of practice made me perfect in that art; and I found it far less shattering to my self-esteem than asking would have been.

Our three meetings called for far more contrivance, but we managed them. And each time we came together with an overwhelming shock of reunion which more than ever convinced me—not that much conviction was needed—

75

that if only we had the money to enable us to live together in moderate comfort and freedom from worry, we should be happy as few couples ever have the capacity for being. Each time when the hour came for me to tear myself away and go back to the Chimney House the prospect seemed so dreary and impossible that I begged Antonia to let me stay with her. Let Eloise divorce me or not, I would cry. We'd been fools long enough. We'd tried setting money before love and look where such a choice had landed us. Antonia only jeered.

'You talk that now, in this comfortable bedroom, paid for with Eloise's money; full of good food provided by the same unwitting woman! You *are* a fool, Dickon, not to see what love in a corner house and on the Underground would end in. We'd hate each other in a week. Do I have to point that out every time we meet?'

'You might hate me,' I was forced to admit, 'but I love you more than that. After all, it was you who left me first. I shouldn't have married Eloise if you hadn't married Joshua.'

She shrugged her shoulders. 'Too true! But I can't see how the situation has altered. You hadn't any money then, and you haven't any now. The only difference is that we're older; and if getting into the sere and yellow doesn't bring you wisdom, at least don't let it soften your brain. Rouse up, my dear boy, and get back to Copham while your alibi holds and I'll go and see what delightful surprise the Helpers have in store for me this bright morning.'

I could never shake her.

So the four years went by in exile from all I cared about. At the end of them—in, that is, the seventh year of my marriage—three things happened almost at once.

First Diana, the child, was taken dangerously ill. A common cold, despite Nanny's nostrums, turned into pneumonia. A trained nurse was installed, but neither Eloise nor Emma Plume could trust her to do anything. Poor woman, she was affronted and almost on the verge of revolt for the whole of the time she was with us.

The second thing grew naturally out of this. Eloise, deprived of her sleep and neglectful of her food, lost what sanity remained to her and began to behave in a highly peculiar fashion. She complained of constant noises in a house that was hushed to deadly quietude; she stopped the clocks; Diana's bantams were banished to the farthest corner of the paddock; the tradesmen's vans were stopped in the road and all goods brought to the house by men on foot. Her conversation—if such it can be called—took on a religious flavour. If God would just be merciful and forgive her and restore Diana to health He should never again have cause for offence. Charities and missions should be cherished as never before and three beds should be endowed at the local hospital in the name of Diana Curwen.

Set down coolly like that, it all sounds like the natural anxiety of a loving parent, but it was worse than that. There was a queer unwillingness to be comforted; and when I told her that Dr. Bethune had said that the child was definitely out of danger she was neither relieved nor credulous. She accused me of hard-heartedness, of being an unnatural parent because I was not displaying a similar extravagance of emotion and because I would not wear slippers in the house all day or speak in whispers and because I occasionally talked to the disgruntled nurse whose presence Eloise resented and to whom she referred, again biblically, as 'a hireling shepherd.' I tried to point out that I was the only person who had addressed the poor woman civilly and that I had, countless times, talked her out of her determination to leave the house in a huff. At the first hint of reason Eloise flung herself into one of her fits, more violent and lasting than any one before. Owing to her recent self-destructive manner of living, this fit ended in genuine un-consciousness, and when she had been carried to her bed I gained the only approval that I have ever had from Emma Plume by announcing firmly that Eloise must consult the doctor on her own behalf. I begged her help. 'If we both insist, she is bound to take notice,' I ended. She relaxed sufficiently to say:

'Well, I'm glad indeed to hear you say so. I've thought the same for a long time, but of course my saying it wouldn't mean so much.' Double-faced old harridan! She knew that her opinion was worth twice as much as mine with Eloise any day. However, it seemed to be left to me to tackle Eloise, which I did as soon as an opportunity presented itself.

It came very soon. I had grown used to Eloise coming out of a sulk by appearing at dinner in a new dress; so I was not really surprised when, the night after the scene, she came down, wearing for the first time a black velvet gown, high-necked and with long close sleeves, out of which her hands and face seemed to emerge more white and ghastly than ever. There were sprays of silver trimming about it too, especially on the skirt.

We carried on one of our slightly self-conscious and totally insincere conversations throughout the meal, and then, since the evening was cool, drew chairs near the fire. Into the pause which had broken the conversation as we left the dining-room I dropped my suggestion that she let Dr. Bethune overhaul her. She looked at me like a spaniel whose master is of uncertain temper.

'Do you care what happens to me?' she asked. 'I didn't know.'

'But of course I care,' I said soothingly.

She slipped out of her chair and knelt on the rug before the fire. Her thin hands fluttered out and found mine, clasping them.

'Oh, say it again, Richard. Say you care. I've been so unhappy all this while. You've been hating me so.' I held her hands firmly, trying to steady them. I beat down my distaste for her emotion, trying to speak warmly, while really I felt as remote as Everest.

'Don't you see,' I asked her, 'that much of the misery has been in your imagination? You've imagined that I hated you. And it's only because you're not well. Old Bethune has done wonders with Diana, hasn't he? And he'll give you a tonic, and perhaps suggest a diet that will build you up a bit, and then we'll take a holiday and everything will be all right again.'

She looked at me oddly, her head held down and her eyes lifted to me, sideways and upwards under their lids.

'Perhaps you're right,' she said. 'Perhaps I do imagine things. All those voices. Sometimes they tell me how wrong it was of me ever to have Diana. She's bound to suffer. She'll fall in love, and meet with disappointment, and be ill at times. And there are all sorts of accidents. And something might happen to the money so that she might have to work, be a servant or a shopgirl. And after all that there's the getting old, and dying alone. You've got to be alone at the very end even if someone is holding your hand. You've no right to put such a burden upon another human being just because you want a baby yourself. It's very wrong. The voices say so, and I know they're right. And yet you, Richard, you say it's all my imagination. What am I to believe?'

The strange look deepened in her eyes. I thought, 'So this is the kind of thing that goes on in that poor tormented mind, is it?' And I was about to say something as sane and comforting as I could think up at such short notice when suddenly she pulled at her hands. I held on, vaguely feeling that I could steady her by my grip. But she cried out as though I were hurting her. So I let her go and she sprang

79

to her feet and stood by the fire with the dancing flames lightening her face and hands and being swallowed in the unreflecting surface of the velvet.

'Don't say it,' she said in a voice that I had never heard from her before, cold and sharp and brittle. 'Don't hand me a dose of philosophy about the world being a pleasant place on the whole and most people enjoying life and being glad they're born. It isn't true. The world is foul and horrible, and things are done in it that only a person like you would be able to ignore. Look at us! A model couple somebody called us. Lucky Mrs. Curwen with her nice house and her sure income and her loving husband! And you married me for my money. Yes, you did. It's the voices speaking now, Richard, and they always tell the truth. I knew on our wedding night. But I thought that you might learn. I tried to be patient. And what was my reward? That you should betray me, under my very roof. I've been a good wife to you, and a good mother to Diana. There's nothing I wouldn't do for either of you. But you hate me. You wish me out of the way. I know. The voices tell me things, true things. Then you could go to that bitch. Because she won't have you without money, will she? I know her. My money and her body. That's what you want. I'm like God these days, I can read your very heart. . . .'

Her voice, which had grown louder and shriller with each succeeding word, broke suddenly. Her fingers strayed to the silver filigree on her skirt and she ripped it, pulling out yards of it, breathing all the while like an over-driven horse.

'I'll call Nanny,' I said. 'You're overwrought.' I could think of nothing else to say. She looked crazy, she sounded crazy, she was crazy.

She rounded on me. 'That's the way,' she cried. 'Run away from the truth. Stop your ears. You've broken my heart and you've spoiled my life and then you call Nanny.'

A gust of maniacal laughter shook her, as one of the silver threads came to an end and hung from her fingers like a slim silver snake. She went on laughing, and then a sob broke through the laughter, followed by another and another. I couldn't have touched her for worlds. It was like watching somebody with leprosy. I began to go to the door, but it opened before I reached it and Emma Plume bustled in with a creaking of starched linen.

'There, there,' she said, putting her arm around Eloise's waist and drawing her towards her. 'There, my lamb. Nanny's here. Nanny won't let anything hurt you. Steady then, that's right.' She patted and fussed her, glaring at me now and again. I threw out my hands.

'That's the result of my saying that I thought she might consult Dr. Bethune,' I said, and walked away to join the whisky in the dining-room.

Nevertheless, next day Eloise herself suggested that Dr. Bethune should come and give her a thorough overhaul. At the end of it he joined me in the library and over a glass of sherry tried to break the news gently. Vaguely and somewhat contradictorily he informed me that my wife was in a bad way but that there was nothing really to worry about. She had a very highly strung and unbalanced nervous system and had overworked herself during the child's illness. The very worst thing was that her heart was extremely jumpy. 'You must, above all things, guard her against any sudden emotion, or any shock of any kind. A narrow escape in motoring, for example, the kind of thing that happens every day almost unnoticed, might easily prove fatal to her. Mind you, I say "might." In these cases predictions are dangerous and I have often found that a—shall we say flawed?—constitution is surprisingly resilient. So I don't wish to give you cause for worry, merely to urge you to care. You have a jewel, of course, in that Nanny.'

He blithered on, cancelling out each statement by the

next. But he had given me cause for worry. If such a small thing might finish off Eloise at any moment my position was far from secure. Little as I was now interested in her well-being, unhappy as our life together had become, I must still preserve, by all means in my power, her life. I must try to avoid those horrible scenes, which, although not of my making, exactly, were yet to do with me.

And immediately on top of this I heard from Antonia. She was nearer to Copham than she had been since she left our house, installed at Sandborough as manageress of The Flitch, an old coaching inn that had been bought by a local syndicate and turned into a luxury seaside place with its own golf links and foreshore. Sandborough was about thirty miles east of Copham and Eloise and I knew the place well; we had sometimes gone there for meals in the previous summer. Antonia mentioned, in the course of her long and enthusiastic letter, that we had not met for almost a year, that she had angled hard for the job in order to be within reach of me again, and suggested that I should run over and see her as soon as possible.

That was easy. Eloise had entered upon another period of rest and Sandborough was within an afternoon's drive. I went over next day.

The moment that I saw Antonia I knew that I should never part from her again. It was like having a meal after a long famine. For a time it was enough just to see her, to watch her, to hear her and to know that she was within reach.

She was very pleased with her new job and showed me over the place quite proudly. We had tea together in the small room at the back of the office which was her particular sanctum. She told me all that she had been doing and I replied by giving her an outline of happenings at Chimney House, concluding with Eloise's illness and the doctor's

82

warning. Then I asked her, 'And how many lovers have you had, Antonia?'

'One here and there,' she replied with the delightful frankness that we used towards one another. 'But you see, I've come back to you.'

My blood sang. But just as we were getting down to essentials, there came a tap on the door and a head poked round. A voice said, 'Oh, there you are, my dear. May I come in?'

Antonia leapt up and straightened her skirt and patted her hair in a way that showed that she was uneasy. The intruder entered the room and she introduced us, calling me her cousin and informing me that this was Mr. Joel Seaman.

He seemed quite at home. Antonia opened a cupboard and brought out a bottle of whisky, a siphon and some glasses. Then she said, 'Oh yes, you prefer water, don't you?' and made for the door.

'Don't bother, don't bother,' he exclaimed, half rising. 'You're not here to wait upon me, you know.'

But Antonia vanished and when she returned she had re-powdered her nose and plied her lipstick afresh. Meantime Seaman and I had looked upon one another with no very great favour and exchanged a few stilted remarks.

When, after two drinks, the man showed no sign of imminent departure, I rose myself and said, 'Well, I must be getting back. I'm glad to have seen the place and to know that you're so happy.'

'Yes, I am, very happy,' she said, and she looked at Seaman and smiled as she said it. Immediately I knew that there was something between this big red-faced fellow in the loud tweeds and Antonia, and when she said, 'I'll see you off, Dick,' I carefully closed the door behind us.

'Who is that perambulating chess board?' I asked.

'Sh!' she said. 'He's the big noise in the company who've taken over the place. I have to keep on his sunny side. So far I seem to have done it.' She laughed.

She came out into the forecourt where I had left the car. Other cars were beginning to arrive and people were spilling out. Antonia regarded them with satisfaction.

'It's surprising the distance people will come for a meal, isn't it?' she asked.

'Does Chess Board come for a meal?'

'He gets nothing else,' she said definitely. 'Still, a lady must live, you know.'

With that she turned to greet some people who had just arrived, and I was left to go back to Chimney House and Eloise.

However, that was only the first of many visits. Antonia was as sweet as ever and we were soon back on the old footing. The only thing that disturbed my peace of mind during those lengthening spring days was the fact that she seemed anxious that Joel Seaman and I should not meet again.

'He doesn't know that you live near. You probably noticed that I simply said you were my cousin. It's just as well that people shouldn't know everything.'

That warned me, in a way. Antonia was not given to caution except where her amatory exploits were concerned; but it did not prepare me to be told, sometime in May, that Seaman had hinted broadly at honourable marriage and that she contemplated accepting him if he pursued the subject.

We were sitting in one of those swinging seats, of which The Flitch garden was full, all tucked away in secluded places. Antonia was curled up, her slim legs laid out on the striped cover and her slender body, in its yellow silk frock, supine on the cushions. She was smoking and looking out over the lavender hedge at the sea.

'I'm tired,' she explained. 'I'm thirty-two this year and I've never spared myself. It's time I dug myself a retreat. This kind of life, this kind of job, can't go on for ever. I don't say that Chess Board is my ideal of a parfait gentil knight, but he has oodles of cash and a decent house and he's quite mad about me.'

'And where do I come in?'

She shifted impatiently. 'We've had all this over a thousand times, Dickon. We haven't any future. In fact this meeting again has been stupid. We'd just proved that we could live apart. Now we've got to start all over again. Because, for one thing, Joel is terribly jealous. For another, I'm sick of being uprooted, and finally, if Eloise ever got to know that you were seeing me again she'd throw a fit that would finish her off. See?'

I said slowly, 'Suppose, Antonia, I had some money. Would you live with me then?' A sudden ray of pure joy shot through the defences of her well-controlled face.

'That *would* be heaven,' she said.

'And would you take a certain amount of trouble to reach that heaven?' I persisted.

'I'd do almost anything. . . .' Then her face shut again. 'Oh, skip it, Dickon. What's the use of talking? Our ways parted on that night when I told you I meant to marry old Joshua. We've tried to cheat ever since, but this will be the end. I'm sorry, deadly sorry. I didn't know that I had it in me to care about anyone as I do for you. But there's nothing for it but to hug our chains and make sure that they're gilded ones.'

I said, 'I won't come here again. But when you receive a picture-postcard of King's College Chapel with just a silly message scribbled on it, be ready, at all costs and regardless of anyone's convenience, to meet me at the book-shop on the corner nearly opposite at three o'clock on the next afternoon. Will you do that?'

85

'It sounds a pretty futile proceeding,' she said. 'Where's the sense in it?'

'It'll give us a chance to meet quite unobserved and to have a talk, at least.'

'It sounds as if we were planning an elopement.'

I laughed. 'It's too late for that. But a plan is budding in my head. I'll tell you more about it when we keep our tryst. Doesn't that sound romantic?'

I had always had a suspicion that my brain was above the average, and God knows I had never worn it out with a lot of study, or worry, or speculation or philosophy. Beyond just troubling it a little now and again in order to appear to be earning my bread, I had left it pretty fallow. But going home from Sandborough that day, I set it to work and it showed its appreciation of past kind treatment by giving me back a plan, so simple, so daring, so wildly audacious that I went quite dizzy as I contemplated it.

I knew that if I lost Antonia again it would be for good. We were neither of us getting younger: very soon the fires of desire would burn lower and we should grow resigned, then lack even the energy that would enable us to go on trying to cheat our fate. There had been an ominous note in her voice when she mentioned her own age and her weariness of her battle with the world. She would marry old Chess Board and probably make him a far better wife than poor Joshua had found her. And I—I should go or bearing with Eloise's temperament until I too was resigned. I looked down the empty years and saw myself growing older and colder with each passing day until at last I died, having missed the one thing that I really wanted.

I shuddered away from this prospect and regarded the only alternative. The plan was horrible. I admitted that. And it was tricky. A thousand small items had to be considered, a good many people had to be dragooned, unwittingly, into line. Moreover, it was such an original scheme that the field of it was unexplored; I should not be able to consult the experience of other men, or take warning from their errors. But these things did not greatly trouble me. As I thought around the subject a feeling of confidence, almost of inspiration, took possession of me. I could not imagine the plan failing.

The horror of it I did examine more carefully as the smooth miles slipped away; but neither did that deter me. What I planned was necessary, that must be its reason and its excuse—though in my eyes it needed none. And having decided that, I shut out every thought, every scruple, every last remaining scrap of honour and humanity. I must fight this final great battle with the gods with the only weapon I had ever known—my wits. And from that moment I became less than a human being, and more. Between Sandborough and Copham I became a detached, unfeeling, clear-thinking automaton, working according to plan, bound for one end. It was comparable with the state of mind that has taken men into battle, or into dangerous experiments in laboratories. And it incurred the same penalty.

When I had really looked around the subject again, mentally free from the fever that its first appearance in my mind had engendered, and still found no flaw in it, I sent Antonia her postcard and the next day punctually at three o'clock picked her up at the place appointed. We drove out to a pretty little tea-garden by the river. All the way there she talked about the latest development at The Flitch. Apparently some entertaining merchant had bought the foreshore rights bang next to the hotel and was setting up a holiday camp there. Men were working day and night and the place was to open with a crash on August Bank

87

Holiday. After months of secrecy the thing had been given immense sudden publicity and already people who had booked at The Flitch were cancelling their reservations, since the whole charm of the place would be ruined by the proximity of the proletariat on holiday. The syndicate was greatly concerned, and Joel, its mouthpiece, had already talked of cutting down expenses.

'I shall be the first to go,' said Antonia, 'because after all I'm only a bit of trimming. I'm supposed to be a kind of hostess and lend the place its dubious tone. If it drops socially there's the old girl who runs the kitchen and staff and she's quite capable of managing it. Joel has said as much, though his manner implies that I have no cause for anxiety. He even had the goodness to inform me that the failure of The Flitch wouldn't do him any material damage.'

'Has he actually proposed to you yet?'

'Not in so many words. It's rather like Joshua all over again, isn't it?'

'Except that this time I have a definite proposal to make myself.'

'Acceptable?' she asked, tilting her head at me.

'That's for you to say.'

I parked the car and we settled down at the most secluded table, under a tree where the little green apples were already forming. The waitress brought the tea and went away. Then I said:

'Antonia, what I have to say sounds very mysterious and I have no doubt you will scoff at it. But if you will just be patient and trust me a little while, everything will be marvellous. I have in my head a perfectly good scheme that demands your co-operation, in a way, but not your help. If it fails, you will be no worse off. In fact you may then marry Chess Board and take my blessing with you. But if it works, and you do as I tell you without asking a lot of questions, you shall live with me on the fat of the land for the rest of your life. The question is, will you do it?'

Over her tea-cup her eyes met mine, level, and for once quite serious.

'What is it?' she asked at last. 'You sound different, Dickon. You *are* different. You almost make me believe that you've got an idea. But listen—if you're going to beg Eloise to let me come back to Chimney House, forget it. She wouldn't have me, and I wouldn't come, that's straight.'

'It isn't that. It's something infinitely better than that, and simpler.'

'Living with Eloise hasn't by any chance driven you nutty too, has it?'

'I don't think so, though it might be calculated to.'

'Then you've come into some money and have persuaded her to divorce you. Oh, Dickon, you might have told me!' Her face lighted. It was quite hard to have to quench the light by saying, 'No. It isn't that. I told you, didn't I, that I couldn't tell you what it was. I have to work it out, you see. But I just want you not to do anything about Chess Board. You needn't give him a downright refusal, just keep him waiting; you know how if anybody in this world does. That's all, except that I want you to be ready to come anywhere at the moment that I send for you.'

Very slowly she refilled both our cups. Then she said:

'It all sounds so simple, Richard. But I have a feeling that it isn't. There's something rather . . . well, ominous about it. I can't see what you're aiming at. Couldn't you tell me a little more? Please, just to ease my mind.'

Fortunately I was well aware of her wheedling ways, and so was armed against them.

'I can't tell you anything more,' I said. 'But I will explain everything in time, and then you'll be sorry if you haven't kept an easy mind. But there's absolutely no cause for worry. As I said before, if the scheme fails you can marry

Joel. Come on now, I have to get back. I'll drop you at the station.'

For the first time in all our acquaintance I was anxious to cut short a meeting with Antonia. I wanted to get away from the risk of more questions. I realised, only too well, that the whole thing must sound most tantalisingly mysterious to her and dreaded that she might say, 'Unless you make things a bit clearer I shall go back to The Flitch and lever a proposal out of Chess Board.' My anxiety not to be questioned overcame even my desire for her and I was willing to leave her with no more than a hand-clasp.

'As soon as things clarify a bit I will telephone you and probably ask you to meet me again,' I said. And then, as though I had just thought of it, not as though the words hadn't been forming and re-forming in my mind, I added casually, 'Oh, and there's one thing you might do, just to please me, Antonia, nothing to do with the other. Grow your hair a bit, that rolly bob is definitely outdated.'

'Good Lord,' she said, startled. 'I must be slipping if it takes you to point out a thing like that. I'll attend to it at once, sir.'

I went back to Copham and lived as usual until one day I waylaid Dr. Bethune at the end of one of his visits to Eloise. In a very subtle way, without saying much, I managed to get from him the admission that Eloise would greatly benefit from a complete change of air and scene. Sea air, he thought, and that would do the child good too. When he had committed himself I said off-handedly:

'Of course it's easy to say such things, but, as you know, my wife is not the easiest person in the world to persuade; look at the way she behaved over that nurse in the spring. She's very much attached to this place, and if I start pointing out that it lies low and is cloaked in by trees she'll probably think that I am tired of it myself, and then nothing will move her.'

'It would probably come better as a professional suggestion from me,' he said.

'It certainly would,' I admitted.

At first, as I expected, Eloise resisted the idea. She didn't feel well enough to consider any upheaval. Diana could go to the sea with Nanny and perhaps she might go and spend a week with them some time. I took no hand in the matter, merely saying, 'Please yourself, my dear.' But after a day or two I let fall the information that Antonia was at Sandborough and feeling very lonely and wondering whether Eloise and I would go over to help cheer her up.

'I shan't,' said Eloise with a glint in her eye. 'But I suppose you will.'

'Not unless you wish me to. You remember The Flitch, don't you? It's only about thirty miles away.'

That simmered for two days and then Eloise herself suggested letting the Chimney House and taking one by the sea for a while. She seemed very grateful when I offered to take the responsibility of finding something suitable and of supervising the move.

In the house-hunting line I seem to be fortunate. I had found the Chimney House, and now, seven years later, I fell upon Moat Place by the merest accident. I had seen several houses which were, for one reason or another, unsuitable, and was actually returning from an abortive trip, when I went into a village pub for a drink and overheard a conclave of village elders regretting that the London gentleman hadn't taken the old Moat after all. It would, they were agreed, have done the village good and helped trade to have had 'the gentry' up there again.

I made a few inquiries, sent Eloise a telegram and spent the night on the most hideously lumpy bed in the pub's spare room. Next day I went to view the London gentleman's leavings and knew that if I had had the place built and dropped into position I could not have arranged anything better.

The village, named St. Brodric, but most often called Broddy, lay at sea level in a dip in the cliffs. To reach the house you went half a mile inland along the road and then took a by-road that led back to the sea at an angle. The by-road climbed gently between fields of thin corn and scanty grass and ended with two posts from which the gate had long since mouldered. Beyond the gate there was a mere track that wound up between blackberry bushes, gorse and stunted hawthorns, until it reached the summit of a fold in the earth. When you topped the rise you could see the house standing on what looked like a ledge of the cliff's face. It was one of the most secluded and least accessible places I have ever seen. But it had great charm. It was so solid and weathered and well-built. The man who showed me round told me that it was well over four hundred years old and that once, before part of the cliff had fallen, the site had been occupied by a fortified and moated castle. On the landward side of it there was a deep depression that might have been the moat. It was now a garden, overgrown, but attractive. The house itself was built of grey stone slabs and had mullioned windows. It was not as pretty as the Chimney House, but it had a grandeur and an outlook that our present home entirely lacked.

Professing doubt and diffidence over my find, I brought Eloise to view it and she fell in love with it at once. We therefore got into touch with the owner, an eccentric fellow who refused to let it, though he was anxious to sell it and quite willing to admit that standing empty improved neither the house nor its value. However, the price he asked was modest and Eloise had set her heart upon it, pointing out that it would make a good house for holidays and that it needed little in the way of repairs. Its plumbing was

92

rather old-fashioned, but it worked, and the four main rooms were so beautifully panelled that it would have been a pity to touch them.

An order to the local builder and decorator for whitewash, distemper, paint and minor things like hinges and doorknobs convinced the native populace that the halcyon days had begun. The baker, the butcher, the grocer and the news agent professed themselves delighted to climb the road and the private slope, known as the Lanes, in order to deliver their wares. My popularity in the village pub when I dropped in during my visits of supervision was amazing.

Although I was attending to everything I often drove Eloise over so that she might see how the work was progressing. During this time I grew more than ever convinced that the wrong people always have the money. If she had been a poor woman, forced to work for her living, her neurosis would have been kept within bounds and probably disappeared. She seemed to be delighted to climb upon a backless kitchen chair and measure windows for curtains, or to pace out a floor to decide upon the amount of carpet needed. Her spurts of energy were short, it is true, and usually ended in extreme exhaustion, but her mind was steadier and at times she went for a week without having a fit. Once, in an unusually friendly moment, she confided in me that the change was just what she wanted. Smothering a pang that was unworthy of the purposeful automaton that I had become, I agreed with her.

'You have a dreadful tendency to get into a rut, you know, my dear,' I said kindly. And passed on from that to the question of taking servants with us.

We had let Chimney House, and what furniture we didn't require at Moat Place, to a Major Morrison who had recently retired from the Indian army. He had several friends in and around Copham and was delighted to get such a pleasant and well-appointed house without being forced to buy. The Morrisons were quite anxious to keep the cook that we had then and she was eager to remain because she was 'walking out' with the postman. Ted, whose home was in the village, never contemplated coming with us. Woods the parlourmaid, Alice the housemaid, and a queer little creature called Dolly, who divided her time between kitchen and nursery, were not yet decided. The plan insisted that not one should come with us. But it was unwise of me to say so. It would only have made Eloise more set upon keeping them.

Woods was the most likely to accompany us, I knew that. She was a tall, well-set-up girl of about eight and twenty, and an ideal parlourmaid. She came from Bedfordshire and had no attachments in Copham. She was alert and intelligent and pretty quick-tempered. She was fond of Eloise, who often gave her clothes that had been worn only about twice.

I set to work on this problem. There was just one small hope. Woods and Emma Plume did not get on too well. There was a certain amount of jealousy, I believe, about Eloise, between them, and Emma, who had old-fashioned ideas, regarded the girl as pert and uppity. This jealousy, I told myself, might be fanned.

One day Eloise was sorting out some clothes. There was to be a jumble sale in aid of the church funds very shortly and she was combining the clearing out before the move with the selecting of stuff to send to it. She had suggested that I should do the same, and the whole of our floor looked like a second-hand shop.

Eloise shook out a pale grey suit trimmed with caracul. She had worn it only once and thought it a depressing colour. She paused now with her head on one side and considered it.

'I was a fool ever to buy this. It looked quite different

then. I believe that shop had rose-coloured lights. It's really rather too good for the jumble. I think I shall give it to Woods. She admired it once, I remember, when she cleared out my cupboard and I did half promise it to her.'

I looked at it contemplatively. 'Why not give it to Nanny?' I suggested. 'It's just her colour and practically new. I believe she'd like it. You hardly ever give her any of your things.'

Eloise looked pleased, and at the same time doubtful.

'I know,' she said, 'but I somehow don't think of Nanny as a servant. More like a friend. I do give her things, but new ones. Still, this is nearly new. I will.'

She laid it aside and next Sunday morning I had the immense satisfaction of watching Nanny go proudly off to church in the pale grey suit while Woods looked balefully down from an upper window. That prepared the way.

It was Woods' duty to see that the trays were set for the nursery meals which were carried up by Dolly. A little butter on a handkerchief smeared over the silver and the glasses, a pinch of dust in the saltcellar, a dead leaf floating on milk made Nanny protest to Woods. Woods, whose work was always perfectly performed, carried the complaint to Eloise, and Eloise, who could never deal with anything, muddled the whole thing, had them both in to see her together, broke down and cried and then collapsed on Nanny's starched bosom. Three more mutilated trays brought Nanny into the fray again with accusations of spite against the parlourmaid, and this time the girl came to me. 'I can't go on like this. Nobody's ever complained about my work before and it's no use speaking to the mistress.'

I soothed her expertly and agreed that in her mistress's eyes Emma Plume could do no wrong.

'If this has only just begun I should think it means that Nanny doesn't really wish you to accompany us to the new

95

house, you know. It'll probably all stop when she finds that you are determined not to come. Old servants are funny in many ways . . . and jealous.'

'Much she's got to be jealous about,' the girl said bitterly. 'And she needn't fret her fat about my going where I'm not wanted. Will you please to take my notice for the end of the month?'

'If you really wish it, of course. But I shall be sorry to lose you,' I said. 'It's nice to see a bright face about, you know.'

'I'll be sorry to leave you, too, sir,' she said warmly, 'but there're limits to everything. Three times in the last week she said the silver was a disgrace. It's my belief she did it herself.'

'I've certainly noticed nothing wrong with the silver at our table,' I volunteered.

'I should hope not. So you'll take my notice, sir?'

'If I must. And look here . . . with best wishes and all that.' I pushed a note into her hand.

I advised Eloise not to risk another upset by inquiring too closely into Woods' motives for leaving.

Dolly finally decided to remain at Copham because her girl friend had only just taken a place to be near her and it seemed 'unkind,' she explained, to leave herself so soon, before the other girl had had time to make any new acquaintances; but Alice stuck like a leech. She wouldn't bother to look for a new job because when she did leave she meant to marry Bob Soames, a garage hand in the village. Where she was for the remainder of her term of service was quite immaterial to her.

I sorted out Bob Soames from the other fellows who worked there and next time I stopped for petrol accosted him jocularly. 'I'm afraid we're taking your lady love rather far away,' I remarked. 'You'll have to come over one Sunday and spend the day.'

He looked gloomy and rather sullen. 'Ass a pity,' he said, 'I doan't like her gawn an thass a fact. But though we got are eye on a cottage we ain't saved enough for the furnichure an we muss wait till Chrissmuss, I reckon.'

'Well,' I said, 'we'll look after her for you. And look here, Bob, I always meant to give you a wedding present. If I get away I may forget, so you'd better have it now. I hope, when it does come off, you'll be very happy. Don't wait too long, there's many a slip you know. . . .'

He looked so concerned at that that I was able to get away before he unfolded the ten-pound note that I had given him with my best wishes.

When I got home I told Eloise that Alice's young man had told me he was hoping to marry her at Christmas and was rather concerned about furnishing the cottage. Eloise sent for Alice and gave her a list of things that we were not anxious to take with us or to leave with the house, just bits and pieces out of the kitchen and nursery. When Alice returned from her next evening out she was all flushed and tremulous and came round the corner of the house to where we were sitting on the terrace as though she had wings. Please, she began, might she tell us? Would we mind very much if she didn't come with us? Bob had suggested that they should get married right away. She felt awful, especially after we had been so kind to her and all. We gave her our blessing.

'Do you realise,' said Eloise, turning to me, 'that that leaves us without a servant of any kind?'

I realised it all right.

'We'll have new ones and start everything afresh,' I consoled her. 'St. Brodric is a completely unspoilt, almost feudal place. I dare say there's quite good girls to be picked up there. Anyway, you leave all that to me.'

'You've been very good about this whole business,' she said. 'I should never have managed it alone.'

'Aha,' I retorted lightly, 'you revile your old husband, but, you see, he has his uses. And by the way, I have another idea. Scotch it if you don't like it. I think that while we are packing up and moving and settling into another house it would be as well to have Nanny and Diana out of the way. You know what a house that has been empty is like. It needs living in before it's really warm and habitable. We don't want to take any risks with her yet, do we? I suggest that we hire rooms, say at Cromer or Hunstanton, and let Nanny take her there at once. Then we can move in peace and have them follow us after a week or ten days when everything is settled.'

'That's really a good idea,' said Eloise. 'She'll be at the sea all the sooner and of course she's as safe with Nanny as she would be with us.'

So far so good. But Emma Plume, as usual, tried to fling a wrench into the works by suggesting that Miss Eloise should also avoid the upheaval by going with them to Hunstanton. And Eloise, who really rather enjoyed the upheaval part of it, immediately wilted and weakened and seemed inclined to give in to the old woman. However, I solved that by appearing to agree that it was a good idea; and then somehow Antonia's presence at Sandborough was mentioned again, and Eloise decided to stay with me.

The plan was working.

Towards the end I spent most of my time at St. Brodric supervising the last of the work and the two women whom I had engaged to scrub and set things straight before the furniture was brought in. On one of these days I telephoned to Antonia, telling her to take a bus from Sandborough on the next afternoon and to meet me by a certain crossroads. I had to drive pretty hard to do it and get back again without arousing suspicion, for Eloise and I were going to Mrs. Campbell's for a farewell dinner and I had promised to be early.

The shortness of our interview was to my advantage, however, for it gave Antonia less time to question me.

Her hair was already knobbed up and netted, though that was less on account of its length than a tribute to Antonia's flair for never looking untidy or 'between styles.'

'Now,' I said, when I had greeted her. 'Everything is working well. We're moving to a place called St. Brodric on Wednesday week. I want you to give in a quick notice at The Flitch. If they make any bones about it give them a month's money. Here it is, and more. You'll need some. Say—be particular about this—that you're not feeling well. Then go to St. Brodric so that you get there on Wednesday too. There's a woman called Mrs. Baker who lives at Myrtle Cottage. She lets lodgings and she has a bath and a telephone—but don't mention that I told you so. Live there, just ordinarily, until I telephone you and ask you to come up to the house. I can't tell you when that will be, but it will be soon. So stay within call for a day or so. When I ask you to come up, you're to take the station taxi, as it is called. It belongs to an old man named Lorkin. He'll drive you as far as the gate, where I want you to get out and walk to the house.' I drew on the ground a map of the by-road and the grassy lane and the gate and marked the position of the house. 'Walk up to the house and that is all you have to do. Oh, all but one thing. Do you think you could possibly persuade a doctor that you had a weak heart?'

Antonia knit her brows.

'I should think so. There were some tablets I once took for sleeping. They knocked you clean out and gave you marvellous dreams, but next day your heart bumped if you so much as ran upstairs. They were meant for women who can stay in bed half the day, and as I was working at the time I couldn't take any more. But I have them still. I should think, if a doctor didn't know anything about them, that he'd think you were in the last stages. . . . But, Dick, I don't see . . .'

99

'Just a minute,' I said. 'At Brodric there's an old doctor called Adams. I've seen him in the pub. Quite a character and about ninety years old. It shouldn't be difficult to foozle him. Go and see him as soon as you arrive. Tell him that you're nervous about your heart.'

'But, look here, Dick. I can't do any of these things unless I *know* why.'

'Very well then, I'm afraid you'll have to stay at The Flitch and marry Chess Board. Has he asked you yet?'

Her face hardened.

'Once he was going to, but I put him off and I think he was annoyed. Now he seems off me and doesn't come in any more. And I've been warned that I shan't be required after the end of August. But that doesn't mean, Dick, that I'm going to play some hokey-pokey game of yours without knowing what it's all about. Going to a doctor about my heart, indeed! You aren't by any chance going to kill me, are you?'

She looked at me with her beautiful eyes and I could see the real doubt and fear in them.

'You know perfectly well that I wouldn't hurt a hair of your head, silly.'

'Then you're going to kill Eloise,' she said, and her hand flew to her mouth and the fear in her eyes screamed at me.

'I swear I am not going to touch Eloise.' I thought rapidly. 'Would it pay me? When Eloise dies the money goes into trust for Diana. I happen to know that.'

'What are you going to do, then? Oh, Dick, you frighten me. I'm sure you're planning something awful and trying to make me help you.'

'Use your sense,' I said quite roughly. 'I've asked you to give up a job that is ending on you anyway and to take a restful little holiday in a village by the sea and one day to come up and see us at our new house. Now what is there awful in that?'

'But it's all part of a plan. You said so yourself.'

'But that is the plan. You were crazy to know what it was and now you say it's awful.'

'Well, if that's the plan, then you *are* mad. You said something about my doing as you told me and then we would live together on the fat of the land. Then you ask me to dinner or something and say that is the plan. It's crazy. Or else you are going to do something to Eloise.'

'I swear to you that I am not going to lay a finger on Eloise. I'll swear that by the love I have for you, which is the only sacred thing I know.'

'Then how can we live together?'

'You'll see. It's rather like a process of legerdemain, and such a process is never explained beforehand. Now, are you coming on Wednesday or not?'

She looked at me again, her beautiful face all broken up with bewilderment and uncertainty. We had wandered quite away from the road and after a quick glance round I stopped, took her in my arms and began to kiss her. She was cold and stiff at first, but soon she was pliant within my arms and returning my kisses warmly. Unwillingly I dragged myself away.

'Now, will you come? There's nothing to fear and nothing to worry about. That I will swear to you. And afterwards everything will be heavenly. Just trust me for this little time, darling, *please*.'

I knew by the expression on her face that I had won.

'I'll come,' she said. 'I suppose it's no dafter than lots of things I have done.'

I drove like a madman back to the Chimney House.

It was an easy move because, since we were leaving some of the furniture, we were able to sleep in comfort on the last night, and as the cook was remaining behind even our meals were normal. Eloise and I set out immediately after lunch, and as I drove slowly and we stopped for tea, we did not arrive until evening.

I have never known a place so quiet. Except for the gentle wash and drag of the waves, far below on the shingle, and the far-off plaintive crying of some sheep, not a sound was to be heard. The women, Miss Footer and Mrs. Roach, had set things more or less straight and left fires in every room. The windows were all warm with firelight when we arrived.

As I unlocked the door I said, 'Eloise, I have been keeping one thing from you. I haven't managed to get any servants yet. But I'm on the track of some and I have found two very good women who will come in every day until we are suited. I thought it best not to hurry. I didn't tell you before because I thought you would worry.'

She took it far more calmly than I had expected. We wandered about, surveying our domain and suggesting improvements for the placing of certain bits of furniture, then I made a scratch meal and we went to bed. I did not sleep very well.

Next day I insisted that Eloise should stay in bed till lunch-time. And now that the move was actually made, her burst of energy seemed to be gone, so she stayed placidly there until the afternoon, when I took her for a short walk along the cliff and then rigged a canopy chair in the garden so that she could rest and get the air at the same time. I wanted to keep her out of the way of the Roach and the Footer, who were busy about the house. At the end of the day I paid them generously and said that my servants were expected on Friday, so I should not want them any more. I promised that any extra cleaning and the household washing should always be theirs. They went off quite cheerfully.

When they had gone Eloise, heartened by a glass of sherry, took revived interest in the house and insisted upon moving some of the smaller things from one room to another and we spent a long time hanging pictures. By eight o'clock we were both dusty and she was out of breath and very tired.

'We'll wash,' I said. 'Then you can sit down while I do my chef act again.'

I collected some food on a tray and carried it to her in the drawing-room.

'My word, it is quiet here,' I said. Eloise shuddered.

'It is. Too quiet. I didn't realise. I wish Nanny and Diana were here, and servants, to liven the place a bit. We'll have to have some people to stay too, shan't we?'

'Not without servants,' I said, keeping my voice light though my heart was going like a drum. 'You see, Eloise, I don't know whether I ought to tell you this, but I don't think we'll ever get servants to stay here, not local ones anyway. I asked Miss Footer—she's the thin one—whether she wouldn't stay in just for a night or two. She said she wouldn't, not for a fortune.'

'Why not?' asked Eloise. Her dilated eyes and trembling voice told me that she knew the answer before I said:

'Oh, some stupid story about its being haunted. Usual thing with a house that's been empty for a while.'

She sprang up, her hands to her breast, and shot a look over her shoulder as though she expected to see Marley's ghost, complete with chains and cash-box, gibbering in the dim corner behind her.

'Oh,' she said, and again, 'Oh. Why did you tell me? Why did we come here? Oh, I can't bear it. I must go away at once.'

'Don't be silly,' I said—but quite pleasantly. 'It's merely a village story. Every village has to have its haunted house just as it has to have a post office. Good gracious, Eloise, you don't believe in ghosts, like a credulous, superstitious kitchen maid, surely?'

'I don't know what I believe. I only know that the mere thought terrifies me. I can't stay here, Richard. I really can't. The thought is appalling. Besides, even if I only *imagined* that I saw something, I should die.'

'You won't *see* anything, even if the old wives' story is true,' I said lightly.

'What is it then, a poltergeist? They're worse. They're evil.'

I filled her glass. 'For goodness' sake, Eloise, sit down and don't agitate yourself. I'm sorry I told you. I was only preparing you for the servant problem. Besides, even if the fiddler does play, it doesn't hurt anybody. Music is harmless enough. It'd be a change from the stuff they broadcast and Diana has on the gramophone.' I laughed a little.

'Who plays? Oh, Richard, you'd better tell me the whole story, otherwise I shall imagine something worse than it is.'

Her terror was pitiable, and I might have pitied her had I any human feelings left, apart from my passion for Antonia.

'It's not an unpleasant story,' I said, pretending not to see that her shaking hand was slopping the sherry down the front of her dress. 'It seems that about two hundred years ago there was a fair in these parts and some gypsies came to it. One of them, a handsome young man, fell in love with the daughter of the people who lived here at the time. He stayed after the fair was over and hung about and made love to her. Her people were proud and her brothers were fierce. He used to come up to her window at night and talk to her, urging her to run away with him. She hadn't the courage or something and never did. But one night the brothers set upon him and threw him over the cliff, I suppose. Anyway, his body was never found, though his fiddle was discovered where he had laid it on that wall that juts out from the end of the house. Soon afterwards ghostly fiddle music was heard around the house at night. The girl, in a frenzy, threw herself out of the window and was killed. The villagers believe that the music still goes on.'

Eloise rose, this time with determination.

'I'm going,' she said. 'Nothing will make me stay in this house for the night. I don't care what we've spent on it, I don't care about anything except getting out of it.'

'Oh,' I said, 'and where do we go? And how? The car isn't running and the village is a good mile and a half away.'

'I don't care. I'd rather sleep in the fields.' And with that she took three determined steps to the door and fell flat. I rushed to her. Perhaps this was the moment. But no, she was breathing. I lifted her and with a mighty effort half carried, half dragged her upstairs, loosened her clothes, laid her flat and applied the remedies that I knew so well by this time. I turned on every light in the room and sat beside her. But she did not need the cheer of light or my presence, she passed straight into sleep. I knew by the change in her breathing and the steadier beating of her pulse. I did not want her to die in the night, so I kept the lights on and slept intermittently in my chair lest she should wake and be terrified again. She slept until morning, when we had another argument about leaving, and I managed to persuade her to wait until next day, when she would be fit to move. I promised that never for a moment during the next twenty-four hours should she be alone, and that we would leave early next day.

The weather had broken overnight and a strong wind was blowing from the west, bringing with it heavy clouds and spatters of rain. I refilled Eloise's hot bottle and persuaded her to stay in bed. This she was willing to do so long as I remained in the room with her, but when I left to go downstairs to fetch some snacks for a rough-and-ready luncheon, she insisted upon coming as well, though she could hardly walk, and dragged along beside the wall, supporting herself by one hand while the other held her dressing-gown clutched close.

I heated some tinned soup and made an omelette. Eloise did not attempt to help; nor did she even inquire where the two women were. She seemed dazed and hardly spoke at all. I poured sherry into the soup and a generous measure of rum into the omelette. Then I persuaded her—for the sake of being fit to travel on the morrow—to drink a glass of champagne. I must make sure that she would sleep during the afternoon and on, if possible, into the early evening.

By half-past three I could see that her eyes were growing heavy and the nervous movements of her fingers becoming quieter. I plumped up her pillows, drew the thick curtains and sat down beside her. Just once, as her eyelids fluttered and she sighed her way into sleep, I had a momentary pang. The complete foulness of what I was about to do unfolded before me and I almost wished that I need not do it. But the wish, the regret, the pang were all fragile things. I had passed the stage where humane considerations could move me. When I thought of Antonia down in the village, so near, waiting for my message to reach her, and pictured what life would be for us when she was really mine, such wild excitement took me by the throat that I could hardly breathe. Beside that prospect the thought of any discomfort or pain of Eloise's counted as nothing.

She was sleeping now and I was able to rise quietly, leave the room and make my last deadly preparations.

So dark and cloudy was the evening that by half-past six the passages were dusk and the curtained room where Eloise slept might have been in the grip of the night. I could not count on her sleeping much longer and the plan demanded that she wake, startled, bemused, alone.

Outside the bedroom, in the thick wall that divided it from the passage, was a cupboard. Softly I stole to it, opened the door and released the gramophone which stood there, ready wound, the chosen record in place. A preliminary scratching sound arose and then the sudden, shrill, sweet yet plaintive notes of the gypsy dance. I drew away, along the dusky passage, and waited.

For a moment there was no sound from the bedroom and then I heard a sharp cry, 'Richard!' It was repeated twice and then swallowed up in a sound that was neither scream nor weeping, a mixture of both, a whimper of terror, a wordless protest against horror. It died away.

The passage where I stood seemed to darken and grow cold. A queer shiver passed down my spine and the back of my calves. A line from some forgotten verse flashed into my mind. 'It's Danny's soul that's passing now.' For a second or two I was unable to move. Not that I wanted to.

I waited. The record ended and I could hear the click as the needle stopped itself. Still no sound.

Now I could walk in and if there were anyone in the room to question or complain I could say that I had been forced to leave her for a moment: dismiss the music as dream or imagination: try something else another day.

But there was no one in the room to question or complain. Eloise had tried to leave the bed. The bedclothes were pushed back but her feet were still entangled in them. She was quite dead. As I had thought and intended, that uncertain heart had not been able to stand the shock of the waking, the unexplained music, the loneliness, the darkness and above all the terror which she herself thrust upon it. I heaped back the bedclothes. There was bound to be a slight time-lag and the question of body heat might, quite conceivably, arise.

Then I went to the telephone.

'Antonia,' I said, 'we're now sufficiently settled to ask you to dinner. Can you come tonight? You can get the taxi that Lorkin meets the trains with. The car isn't running. . . . Good. Don't be long.'

Antonia Meekin

THE telephone at Mrs. Baker's house rang eight times between my arrival on Wednesday and the Friday evening. It caught me each time. Eight mortal times did I think, 'Ah, that's Dickon, now I shall know,' and eight times it was a call for the lodger whom Mrs. Baker called her 'steady' and who sold soap or something that made people telephone him a lot.

But when the bell rang again on Friday evening I was so certain that at last it was the call for which I had been waiting that I was out of the bath and trying to dry myself on the thin small rag that did duty as a bath towel at Myrtle Cottage before Mrs. Baker puffed upstairs to tell me. I went down and stood in the narrow passage that smelt of floor polish and cooking and held the receiver to my ear. I was so excited that my flesh seemed to move on my bones, and it was a definite relief to hear Richard saying in his own normal, laconic voice that they were now settled enough to ask me to dinner.

I said, 'All right. I'll be seeing you,' and went upstairs to dress. I still had that peculiar feeling of not really fitting my skin properly, and it was that more than anything else which made me stop in the middle of doing my hair and ask myself whether I really intended to go up to Moat Place that night. Not for the first time I wondered whether living with Eloise hadn't driven Richard batty. It would have me. That's why I couldn't live in Birmingham with her, restful as that would have been. And I'd only stayed those months at Chimney House because of Richard. And honestly, since that day at Cambridge when he had said something about a plan, his manner had been peculiar enough to warrant the notion that his brain was turned. And yet tonight, speaking on the telephone, he'd sounded quite ordinary.

Hanging on to the memory of his quiet normal voice, I went on making myself ready, wondering what my meeting with Eloise would be like. I had never set eyes on her since the night before the fracas when the brat had croup, and it wasn't really a very sweet position. And with that I paused again. Dickon had said, 'We're sufficiently settled to ask you to dinner,' but did I really expect Eloise to be there? I couldn't give myself any very conclusive answer. Where else should she be?

I realised as I slipped into my dress and began to make up my face that I hadn't given this matter the thought that I ought to have done. I seldom do. Long ago I had realised that thinking never altered anything and that if you once begin you never know where to stop and you start questioning your own motives and those of other people and get into a tangle and lose your grip. I'd come to Broddy because Dickon had told me to and because the job at The Flitch had curled up on me, and I'd had a setback over Joel Seaman. And although I'd been curious and a bit worried over what Dickon was up to, I hadn't really analysed the situation. It was a bit late to start, but while I waited for the station taxi, and bumped along in it and got out exactly where I was told to and walked up that ghastly lane in the dark, I thought over, as clearly as

I could, what I was doing and what Dickon might conceivably have planned.

I'd always had a respect for Richard's brain. Lots of people might think he hadn't any, but they were wrong. He had a cleverness that was almost devilish at times. He could trip you up in an argument, or wangle a way out of a jam in a fashion that was quite uncanny when you considered the stupid way in which he generally behaved. In fact his brain turned on and off, like an electric light, and I had a feeling that for the first time he had turned it on to the subject of us, and God knew what might be the outcome of that. Always before he had just drifted, saying vaguely, 'Let's go away together,' or 'I'll divorce Eloise if you'll marry me,' and taking, like the people the Bible praises so over-highly, no thought for the morrow, what we should eat or what we should wear. You can't live on love, as I'd told him often enough, and I'd had quite enough to do to keep myself, so I'd always dismissed his chatter with the contempt it deserved. Until now. My very bones told me tonight that Dickon was not to be dismissed lightly. I came back to my old feeling about him, that there was nothing he couldn't do if he set his mind to it.

Yet, on the other hand, what could he do? He was married to Eloise and she had the money. If she divorced him he'd be a pauper. If she died, ditto. And yet he had told me that if I obeyed him we should live together and have enough money to be comfortable.

I'm mentally lazy: and I felt inclined to give it up. After all, there are a lot of things that I can't understand. Mathematics, how a camera can take a photograph, wireless, and what makes a car go. Yet there are numbers of people who do understand these things. And in a world where the twisting of a knob will bring you the sound of singing from half a world away I suppose nothing is impossible; so I supposed it wasn't impossible that Dickon should have thought of some apparently simple and workable way out of our little cul-de-sac. He had spoken of a process of legerdemain and I was half inclined to think that there might be something in it. But legerdemain is trickery and as I bumped along in that villainous old bus of a taxi I reminded myself that Richard wasn't a juggler giving a performance before a dazzled audience. He was a man who had married one woman and now promised to live with another. . . .

Frankly I could think of only one way out. And that was that he had had Eloise certified. I shouldn't have blamed him for that. If her mother had been put away in some nice comfortable mental home Uncle Everard would have had a happier life and Eloise might have had a chance to grow up more normal. Perhaps Dickon had thought about the child's future and done what Uncle Everard should have. So perhaps Eloise wasn't up there at the house. . . . And yet Dickon had said *we*. And then too there was that business of my seeing the little old doctor. How did that fit? 'My God,' I thought, 'this is a puzzle and no mistake. Maybe it's I who am nutty. After all, Aunt Ella was my mother's sister, perhaps the mental trouble has broken out on my side in this generation. Perhaps there's something perfectly simple and vital that could explain all these things and I can't see it because I'm haywire myself. Well, at this rate,' I reflected, 'if I'm not now, I soon shall be. I must wait until I am confronted with something that I can understand.' I remembered the shattering sound of that telephone bell and thought of the bells they sound to get theatre audiences to quit the bar in time for the next act. It was like that. I was either going to see, or take part in, the act that was the logical outcome of my meeting with Richard all those years ago. Also, I must admit it, I was excited at the thought of seeing him again. I never knew anybody who got a hold on me as he had done.

I kept a sharp look-out and soon the gate-posts showed and the old man who was driving began to turn the car. I tapped on his shoulder and told him that I would walk up to the house. It was a pleasant night and I should enjoy the air. He seemed very pleased and wouldn't take the full fare which I offered him.

"Oh no, lady,' he said, 'fair's fair, and my old Mary here'll be only too glad not to have to grind up that there lane. She ain't much good off the level these days.'

As I stumbled away up the rough path, ricking my ankle in rabbit-holes and catching my dress on the prickly bushes, I could hear him turning round in the narrow road and then triumphantly grinding away. After that it was so quiet that I could hear my own breath coming in gasps and gulps as I made the grade. Richard had explained the lay-out and I knew that I had to climb to the top.

I'd had no idea that I was so out of form. I had never been one for sweating about playing games, partly because my efforts have mostly been directed at something mildly lucrative, but I'd always been an indefatigable dancer and at The Flitch I'd had to look pretty slippy during most of the day; but tonight I was panting like a grampus and I could hear my heart knocking. For one dreadful moment I wondered whether it was myself, not the doctor, whom I had fooled a couple of days ago. I'd swallowed my tablet the night before and had had the usual heavenly dream and waked up feeling like a wet dish-rag. And after he had tapped and listened he'd told me that I'd got a nervous heart, a bit jumpy and inconvenient but nothing to worry about. He was a nice fatherly old thing, pretty unperceptive but well-meaning. And now, puffing along, I wondered whether his manner hadn't hidden something. It would have been a good ironic situation if through falling in with Dick's plan I now went and died on his doorstep.

All rot of course. I got to the top and stood there for a

minute or two, breathing steadily, and very soon I felt all right again. The slope down was easy and when I had made half of it I thought I heard a sound and stood still and listened. It was Dickon. He came charging through the darkness and said rather quietly, 'Antonia.'

I said, 'Hullo, Dickon. Yes, it's me.'

'So you did come,' he said, and I heard all his breath go out in a sigh of relief.

'You ought to have your path levelled if you want people to walk up it,' I said. 'I pretty near killed myself getting to the top.'

'What?' he asked in a startled voice.

'Have you ever tried to walk it? I thought not. If you had you wouldn't sound so surprised.'

He was dragging me down the slope and in a few seconds we were at the door of the house, which he had left ajar. He pushed it open, let me pass in and then pushed it back and I heard the lock click.

'Let's look at you,' he said, pulling me under the light, and peering into my face. 'You do feel all right now, don't you, Antonia? I'll get you a drink.'

'I'm all right,' I said. I looked round the hall; it was higher and wider and colder-looking than the one at Chimney House and all the bits of furniture that I remembered looked as though they had shrunk. But they reminded me that I was once again under Eloise's roof, and my old doubts as to my reception revived.

'Where's Eloise?' I asked, thinking that I might as well get the meeting over.

'She's dead,' he said, as calmly as though he were saying that she was in the drawing-room.

My skin, which hadn't really fitted me all evening, went goose-flesh right up to my scalp, where I could feel my hair prickling. I wanted to get away from Dick and I wanted something to lean against, so I backed away against a chest that stood by the wall. I heard my own voice say, 'So you've killed her.'

He took a step or two towards me, but I put up a hand that felt like a fin and said, 'Keep away from me, Dickon. It's no use, I do bar murder, astonishing as it may seem.'

'You might wait until the doctor has seen her before you start making accusations,' he said, and his voice was still calm and quiet. 'Meanwhile, if it gives you any comfort, I repeat that I haven't laid a finger on her.'

'You can poison a person without laying a finger on her,' I said.

'And then call in the doctor? Don't be silly, Antonia. And don't waste any more time. Can't you see what the idea is? You're going to be Mrs. Curwen, from now on, and we've got to make it look as though it was you who died through walking too quickly uphill. I'll explain everything afterwards, but just now you must help me. I've got to get the doctor and I mustn't lose another minute.' He laid an urgent hand on my arm. I took his wrist in my fingers and pulled him round so that I could look in his face.

'Did you kill her?' I asked.

His eyes met mine, serene and innocent.

'We'll leave the doctor to answer that. Now, are you going to help me, or spoil the whole thing by wasting time quibbling?'

It was partly curiosity that took me upstairs. Eloise lay in the bed, and she certainly looked peaceful enough. It wasn't a very good moment for me; but I forced myself to go up to her and I bent down and sniffed at her lips. I did it more to show Richard what I suspected than anything else, for I am ignorant as a hog about poison, and only remembered from seeing a play that prussic acid smells of bitter almonds. But I couldn't smell anything and Richard didn't turn a hair, so I was no wiser than before.

For the next ten minutes I obeyed him as though I had been hypnotised, and at the end of them we had finished. Eloise was downstairs, dressed in my clothes, lying on a sofa in the little study just inside the front door. Dick either kept his head wonderfully, or else had the whole thing so well planned that it was like a train running on a familiar line. Even our rings were changed, and my bag lay by her side. There was brandy in a tumbler on the table and a little of it smeared on her mouth. The uncorked smelling-salts stood on the floor nearby. As soon as it was all set he went to the telephone and called the doctor's house. This time his voice did sound agitated.

The doctor wasn't in, but he was expected back soon, and after asking the address of the nearest other one Dick left a message to say that Dr. Adams was to come to Moat Place the very moment he returned. Then he put down the receiver and stood biting on his finger.

'The nearest other fellow lives at Notham. I don't know whether it would be worth trying to get hold of him. I don't think so. After all, he could be expected to know that it was hopeless, and actually the longer we have to wait the better it is, having lost so much time already.'

'While we're waiting perhaps you'll be good enough to tell me exactly what happened. Damn it all, Dick, you've kept me in the dark far too long as it is.'

'She had a heart attack. That's all that happened. You'll see that the doctor will confirm that.'

'All right,' I said. 'If that's all you will say I will wait until the doctor has been. I'm not a bit satisfied. But you must realise that if you're passing her off as me, I am involved, whether I want to be or not.'

'There's nothing to be involved in, I tell you. Look here, Antonia, don't be so suspicious and obstructive. You said you wanted to live with me, and that could only be done on Eloise's money. Therefore we mustn't let anyone know

118

that she is dead. You can see that, surely. But that doesn't mean that I had to kill her. It merely means that we must conceal the fact that she is dead. She died in the most natural way in the world—for her—and it was timely—for us. That's all. Now you get upstairs out of the way. The doctor'll be here at any minute and there's no point in stressing the resemblance. It'd be better if he didn't see you.'

I went upstairs, not into the bedroom from which we had taken Eloise, but into another, nearer the head of the stairs. God knows that I'm the last person to be nervous or indulge in spooky thoughts. Leet was as haunted as any place could be and I didn't mind that a bit. But standing there in that awful silent house and knowing what lay downstairs wearing my clothes got me as jittery as a darky in a ghost film. It seemed to be deadly cold and I shook as if I'd taken an ague.

I was frankly delighted to hear the doctor's car chug up at last and swish to a standstill on the gravel. I heard Dick run to the door and tear it open. I thought for the hundredth time since I had stood there that if he had *done* anything—and at that moment I was willing to suspect him of almost anything on earth—he would never have dared to fetch in a doctor to view that body. He couldn't have. On the other hand, if he hadn't done anything how had he managed that Eloise should die just at the moment that was, as he termed it, so timely for us?

I'm sure I aged ten years, standing there, listening.

Old Adams seemed to recognise Richard and I remembered his saying that they had met in the pub. But he seemed not to have connected him with the telephone call.

'Why, Mr. Curwen,' he exclaimed as he entered the house, 'I didn't realise. Silly of me. Moat Place, of course. I trust it's nothing serious.'

I heard Richard say gravely and rather ponderously, 'Serious enough, I'm afraid. My cousin, Mrs. Meekin, came up to dinner with us this evening and foolishly elected to walk part of the way. She arrived in a state of collapse and though we've done what we could I'm very much afraid that she's dead.'

'Good heavens,' said the doctor. 'Mrs. Meekin? Oh dear, I'm so bad at names . . . but would she be a pretty, red-haired lady who came to me only on Wednesday? She seemed nervous of her heart. It was certainly jumpy, but gave no indication that it might fail so soon.'

Richard said something in answer to that, but I couldn't hear it because they were across the hall by that time and into the study. I suddenly felt that I'd got to know what was said at first-hand, otherwise it would kind of lie between me and Dickon all our days. So, much as I loathe eaves-dropping, I slipped down the stairs and stood outside the study door. By that time I guess the old man had satisfied himself that Eloise was dead—anybody could have seen that with half an eye.

'This must have been a terrible shock for you,' he was saying. 'These sudden passings are always hardest upon the observers. She could hardly have felt anything at all.'

Richard, still speaking in that head-of-the-family sort of voice, said, 'It was even worse for my wife, who is very nervous and not at all strong. I have persuaded her to lie down.'

Maybe because I was conscious of spying it seemed to me that he raised his voice at that, as if he were speaking to me. And not knowing when they might open the door, and being kind of half satisfied because the old man wasn't already ringing up the police, I skipped out of the way and up the stairs again.

I heard the door open and shut and Richard said, as if carrying on from some remark I hadn't caught, 'No. I don't think Antonia banted. I think it was the sharp walk uphill. I'm sorry now that I couldn't fetch her, but my car went wrong yesterday.'

'You mustn't torment yourself with idle regrets. These things happen, you know. Though I must admit that I should have given her several years of life yet if I had been asked to prophesy. But there, there, we all come to it. Oh, and if you'll just give me her full name and so on I'll make out the certificate and perhaps you could call in the morning. And there's a very good woman in the village. . . . I'll send her along, shall I? I'm afraid you'll have to go farther afield for an undertaker.'

Dickon said, 'I'll see to all that. And thank you very much.'

And still, I thought, I don't really know what she died of. I went nearly to the top of the stairs and called down, 'Oh, Dick, what does the doctor say?'

He called back confidently, 'Heart failure. I'll be with you in a moment.' Excellent imitation of husband calming worried wife. I always knew he could have done anything. He could have acted. He could have written. Mainly I think because he could make himself believe anything he chose to.

I heard the exchange of good nights and the shutting and locking of the front door. Then I ran down the stairs again.

'Now,' I said, 'I want to talk to you, my brilliant young man. Lock that other door, for God's sake, and rustle up a drink. And haven't you a fire in this mausoleum?'

'There's one in the kitchen,' he said, opening another door. There were a few miserable embers in the cooking range and Dickon threw on sticks and little knobs of coal and pulled out the dampers. Soon it was roaring steadily and I put out my hands to it, more than a little glad to see something cheerful and feel the warmth of it. He opened a new bottle of whisky and splashed out a couple

121

of drinks into tumblers that he unearthed from a jumble of things on the dresser. I downed mine in one.

'I wanted that,' I said. 'And now, please tell me all about it. How did you kill her?'

'I did not kill her. She died of heart failure. You took good care to make me say that in the doctor's presence, didn't you?'

'Don't talk arrant nonsense,' I said crossly. 'If a person dies to within an hour of when you intend them to you must have had something to do with it.'

'And how do you know that she died within an hour of my intending her to?'

'By your ringing me up. By your having me here. It all fits too well. A cretin would think there was something wrong.'

'I fail to see why.'

'All right,' I said, getting to my feet and hitching up the dressing-gown that he had given me to wear. One of his own; I wouldn't touch anything of Eloise's at that stage. 'If you won't or can't be frank with me I shall go to that doctor and tell him who I am and bring him back to examine Eloise properly.'

'The whole medical faculty might examine Eloise properly, as you term it. And they'd all tell you the same thing. You can go and fetch the doctor if you like. It'll put me in a nasty jam and you'll look a bit queer yourself, and all the good red gold will go into trust for Diana, that's all.'

He positively glared at me, but he didn't look the least like a person who has done a murder that might be found out. I weakened.

'If you'd only be frank with me,' I said.

'But I am being frank with you, darling, only you won't let me tell you. You will keep telling me. Eloise took one of her peculiar fits, hysteria, or mania, or what you will. Nanny wasn't here to hold her hands and exercise her magic charm and she just died. That, darling, is the solemn, the unadulterated and the whole truth.'

Now next to Nanny Plume I think I knew those fits of Eloise's as well as anybody. Even as a child you'd only to cross her, or upset her in any way, and she would cry, quite wildly, and chuck herself about and scream. Four or five good clouts in the early days might have cured her, but she always got wads of attention and sympathy, partly because she was so fair and frail and so gutlessly sweet in between times, and partly because everybody thought about her mother. Which just goes to show you what fools even clever people like Uncle Everard can be. I mean Eloise's mother; my Aunt Ella was nutty as hell, years before that wretched son of hers was born. I know she was my mother's twin and all that, but I believe it often happens with twins, one gets all the beauty or all the brain or all the vice and the other is left without any. My mother, not that I had much chance of judging, seemed to have all the brains of the pair and as long as I can remember Aunt Ella was a bughouse case, only nobody would admit it. So they let her keep about, and even let Eloise go out with her. Which seems to me simply asking for the 'accident,' as they insisted upon calling it, which finally put paid to Eloise's chance of ever growing into an ordinary person.

Not that Eloise was all that crazy. I would have thought twice about foisting her off on Dickon if that had been the case, but she was queer. And in my opinion Emma Plume had made her worse. The woman had what they call a 'power complex' and it simply flourished on Miss Eloise's delicacy, nutty ideas and 'bad spells.' I'd always thought that a husband could have coped with that kind of thing: and I'm certain that a happy marriage would have steadied Eloise a lot. But, of course, she insisted on taking Emma Plume with her, and I suppose Richard wasn't really the ideal husband for her anyway.

123

Still, even so, although I knew about Eloise's temperament and had long ago decided that it was something I'd sooner not live with, I couldn't accept Richard's story without mentioning what seemed to me the one important point.

'What I can't stomach is that you knew it was going to happen. You had the stage all set. Nobody in the house but you. You had me hanging on the end of the telephone. You had me grow my hair. You *knew*, Dick, it's no use pretending you didn't. And if you knew—well, then you did something.'

A very stubborn look came over his face. I knew it well.

'All I knew was that latterly Eloise has taken about two fits a week. I told you that I didn't know the day I should ask you to dinner. You remember that? It might have been a month from now, it might have been six. On the other hand it might have been yesterday. I knew that sooner or later she would excite herself too much. That was all I knew. And on that very small knowledge, you must admit, darling, I have made a neat job. Grant me that.'

'A very neat job. If it works. And if I can bring myself to believe your story.'

'Well, I can't make you believe it,' he said, getting up to refill our glasses. 'But, if you can bring yourself to do so, things can be very pleasant, Antonia.' He had a way of using my name sometimes so that it made my heart turn over. 'And while you are sitting in judgment you might ask your so virtuous self whether you can be absolved from all blame. After all, you played your part, you know. Why was that?'

A very subtle question. And the answer was that I had, all along against my reason and better judgment, *hoped* that he would pull off something that would enable us to live together. For I must admit that Richard was, of all the

124

men I've known, the only one that I wanted to spend my life with. I can't tell you why, except that there was a definite urge. I know that we hard-boiled wenches, especially if we have any claims to attractiveness and haven't exactly lived like Vestal Virgins, are not supposed to have any feelings at all. But that isn't true. After all, if you wanted to know what to choose in a good restaurant you wouldn't consult a food faddist who lived on bread and water, you'd take the advice of an experienced gourmet. And so, when I say that Richard Curwen had got what it takes, you may believe me that he had. Where it lay I don't quite know. He was handsome enough, but I've known better-looking men. He could be cruel and vicious, he was certainly idle and luxury-loving, though Heaven knows I shouldn't count those as drawbacks, and he was selfish. But he could be sweeter than anyone I've ever known, and he brought to his love-making all the vitality that most men squander banging balls about or watching the tape on the Stock Exchange, or toting vacuum cleaners from door to door, if you know what I mean.

But, of course, I wasn't going to tell him that. So when he asked me why I had played the hand he'd dealt me so far I laughed and said that long training had fitted me to do anything I was paid to. 'And what do we do now?' I asked.

'Live here as though you were Eloise. You're not over-particular about the ethics of that, I take it. Eloise's money comes in regularly. There is a lawyer up in Birmingham who handles her business, but to my certain knowledge he hasn't seen her since we were married; so even if circumstances arose in which you would have to see him I don't think it would matter. Seven years and some make-up would account for any difference he might think he noticed.'

'Thank you,' I said. 'I must say that I find your insistence upon the likeness between us most flattering.'

'Well, it is there. It took in the doctor. He just gaped at Eloise and said that he had thought Mrs. Meekin a very pretty young woman but hadn't realised that she was so emaciated. If he had he would have given her a few words of advice about diet. I denied that Mrs. Meekin had banted. I'd hate to suggest that it would take more self-denial than you are capable of.'

'And what,' I asked, 'about signing things? Have you thought of that?'

'My dear Antonia, give me credit for some sense. I've signed cheques with Eloise's name at least four times lately and she never even noticed them herself. If you'll just cheer up and take a sensible view of things you'll see that we're sitting pretty. We'll have to stay here for a bit and you'll have to curb your natural exuberance. You can't suddenly start driving the car or striding about the village, because Eloise's delicacy is already an established fact, partly because I had to keep her out of the way of the hags who came to scrub and help move in. But it needn't be for long. We'll get away from here and start hitting the high spots very soon. And it won't be so bad here when we get some servants. They're just waiting the word to say that we have opened the house. I tell you, I didn't rush into this without due consideration.'

'You're very clever,' I said.

'Once you said otherwise. You said I had no money and no sense.'

'You can be clever without having sense. I'm not admitting that there is any sense in this arrangement. It's a perfectly dopey idea. But now and again somebody is lucky enough to pull off a dopey idea and I hope you will. Here's to it.' I raised my glass.

Dickon came over and perched on the arm of my chair, putting his arms round me and burying his face in my neck.

He began to babble about having done it all for me. That he couldn't live without me. That we'd wasted seven years of our lives and mustn't waste any more. I felt the urge beginning and for the first time began to feel glad that I had cut away from The Flitch and let go the security that old Chess Board offered. And then, just as I was going to kiss him, I had a thought that turned me absolutely stiff. I pushed him away and said, 'What about the child, Richard? And Emma Plume?'

His face went white. 'My God,' he gasped. 'That's the one thing I had forgotten; and they're due in a few days. Not that the child matters. She's not six till next month and she's been away since the first week in July. She'd hardly remember Eloise herself. But that blasted Nanny is another thing. They say people always forget the one crucial point, and this proves the truth of that saying. Still, now you have reminded me, bless you, it'll be easy enough. I'll write her a pleasant letter and explain that Diana is going to have a governess. That'll settle her. I might even send her a cheque to pacify her.'

'You'd better telephone the Helpers' tomorrow. They'll get you a good woman in about half an hour. They keep them in cold store, I believe.'

'And she can pick up Diana at Hunstanton. My God, what a pleasure it will be to have a house without Emma Plume in it. I don't think I've ever detested a woman so much. I always blamed her for the fracas the night the kid crouped. The natural thing would have been to go to Eloise's room first, wouldn't you have thought?'

'Not for her. You'd better write tonight, hadn't you? Before you forget again.'

'That's right. Mock me,' he said. But he got the things and sat down and composed a letter that I thought was really brilliant when he read it out to me. It had that proper pompous fatherly note. When he'd finished writing

127

he hunted about and found Eloise's own fountain-pen to write the cheque with. She always used one of those snub-nosed nibs that write as though they've got a hair on them. I suppose that made it easier.

Next day, of course, there was a lot to do. But he remembered to get hold of the Helpers' and during the afternoon they rang back and said that Miss Myra Duffield was free to come at once. They gave her address and an astonishing list of her qualifications. Dickon wrote off straightaway telling her when and where to meet Diana. He'd fixed it so that the governess and the Nanny wouldn't have a chance to prate.

'The old hag might say something about Eloise that mightn't quite click with the Mrs. Curwen that Miss Duffield is going to find here,' he explained.

'A crafty thought,' I said. 'I congratulate you on it. But I do demand, Richard, that when you tire of love's young dream with me you give me due notice. I'll go quietly. I don't fancy being a bride in a bath—or a mistress in the moat it would be in this case, wouldn't it?'

'You've got a nasty mind,' he said. 'What is more, with your hair in a bundle like that and that horrible suit you look so like the late lamented that I keep wanting to offer you the smelling-salts.'

'I know a better pick-me-up,' I said.

It seemed that the plan was working. The funeral went off without a hitch. I sent myself a whacking great wreath! The sort I certainly shouldn't have had from anybody else. The servants arrived and by the end of the week everything had settled down in such an astonishing fashion that it seemed as though I really had become Eloise and had lived with Dickon for quite seven years.

Two days before Diana was due there came a funny telegram about a donkey.

'It's something that Nanny must have written to Eloise about,' said Richard. 'Have a look and see if you can find a letter. There was one, I believe, just before we left Copham. Eloise never showed me Nanny's scrawls after one I laughed over.'

I searched high and low but could find no trace of it amongst Eloise's things.

'Send her a telegram and tell her to please herself. She'll do that in any case.'

So he telephoned a telegram and when he put down the receiver he said, 'Well, there, thank God, is the end of Emma Plume. A fitting epitaph. "She pleased herself and nobody else."'

Dickon drove down to Notham St. Mary to meet the train and presently came back with Diana, marvellously brown and pretty, but so like Eloise as I remembered her from staying with Uncle Everard that it gave me quite a jolt, and Miss Duffield.

We had arranged that Diana should meet me alone, in case she came out with anything dubious, though Richard was quite sure that she wouldn't know the difference. I wasn't so sure. I'd seen the young deer at Leet pick their own mothers out of a whole herd of does, and I thought that even a child of six might have that much sense. But when the car stopped I lay down in the chair and kind of slumped and ruffled my hair and hoped for the best. Richard sent Miss Duffield to her room and then brought Diana in. I held out my hands and smiled—faintly-sweet like Eloise would—and said, 'Hullo, darling. I'm so glad to see you back.'

The poor little brute looked at me and then at Richard and seemed to shrink into herself. She clung to his hand and wouldn't come a step forward. He pushed her gently and told her to go and kiss Mummy after all this long time

and asked her whether she had forgotten me. I thanked
my stars that she had never known Aunt Antonia. Richard
laughed and said, 'She's forgotten you, Eloise. And she's
brought you such a nice present, too. A white donkey.
That's right, isn't it, Diana?'

Still clutching him and backing away, she said, 'I want
Nanny.' Shades of Eloise!

'But she's having a little holiday. You've had yours. You
wouldn't grudge poor Nanny a little rest, would you?'
Richard asked patiently.

'Besides,' I said, not quite so patiently, 'you're big
enough to do without her now. Mummy'll look after you.
Come along and let me take your coat off. Then we'll
have tea with lots of cakes and you can tell me all about
the donkey."

Propelled by Richard, she came forward and I began to
unbutton her coat. It was just like undressing a doll. She
wouldn't even lift her arms so that I could pull her sleeves
free. I was more than glad that nobody but Richard was
there. I don't think I've ever seen such suspicion on anybody's face in all my life. She looked puzzled, too, and
honestly I did feel sorry for her. And I thought of the
young deer again and realised that if her instinct was
against accepting me for her mother her eyes and her ears
must have seemed to be deceiving her. Suddenly she burst
into tears. I tried to distract her by ringing the bell and
ordering tea, laying great stress on the honey, the cherry
cake and the chocolate biscuits. Just as Norton, the parlourmaid, went out, she said, 'Where's Woods?'

'She didn't come to this house,' said Richard.

Diana cried harder than ever. 'Everything's so funny,'
she said.

Richard—I believe he enjoyed playing father—went down
on his knees and held her in his arms.

'I'm not funny, am I, darling? And Mummy's not

funny. It's only that it's a new house and seems rather strange. You'll be very happy here. There's the beach all the time. And you'll have the donkey. Has he got a name? You haven't told us anything about him, have you?'

At last something had clicked. Certainly this was Eloise's child. The only thing Eloise ever really cared about was animals. She would have given the R.S.P.C.A. her last dime any day. (I made a note that I must continue her subscriptions.) The child told us that the donkey was called Snowball, and more or less explained why she had wanted to buy him, though it was all a curious jumble of sticks and vegetables and meadows. But were we glad of the diversion! And when the tea came Richard plied her so hard with honey and cherry cake that I guessed she'd soon need Nanny's attention rather badly. I had just thought of that when Richard said to me, in French, 'It would be as well if you kept the child away from the governess until there is no doubt left in her mind. I will engage the good lady's attention by being the model father, full of suggestions for schemes of work and time-tables.'

'Hold off anything that might strengthen the memory then,' I said, and prayed she wouldn't be sick.

So for two whole days I took charge of her, washed, dressed, exercised and amused her, while Dickon did his best to conceal his abysmal ignorance of what a child of six should have in the way of educational fare. They were trying days, too. Every now and then I'd catch her eye on me, distrustful, puzzled, questioning. And then, getting well into the second day, a sudden change came over her; from behaving as if she'd been pole-axed and couldn't think why, she progressed to active, fiendish disobedience. I'd had some curious jobs in my time, but I had been spared the young of the species, and I just didn't know what to do with her. I couldn't very well lam into her, which was what she needed and what I wanted to do, because I was supposed to be matching up to Richard in parental affection. So I just gave up and if I wanted her to do anything took care not to say so. Even when that donkey arrived from the station and I thought I really was on a sure thing, she wouldn't let me lift her on to its back; I insisted and then she threw herself down, screaming and kicking, for all the world like Eloise when she was crossed. I said to Richard then:

'Oh, for God's sake, let me pass her on to Miss Duffield. If she'd been going to blurt anything out she would have by now. And if she treats me to any more fits I shall probably strangle her anyway.'

So the governess carted her off to the room Richard had been getting ready, and they took to one another, thank goodness, and were soon as thick as thieves. We had one more delightful scene when we had at last to break it to her that Nanny wasn't coming back. She fell down flat on her face and scrabbled at the carpet and yelled and drummed her feet. I did then what I'd always longed to do to Eloise, caught her one sound smack on the bottom. That stopped it. But Miss Duffield looked at me with such horror and astonishment that I was quite shaken and muttered something futile about that being the best way to cope with hysteria and that I hoped she'd not let Diana grow up neurotic. That gave her something else to think about.

We had one bad jolt. There came a spell of better weather, St. Somebody's summer, and I began to get restless. It was all right being Eloise when the weather was foul, but when the sun shines I like to be out in it. So Richard and I went down the cliff and had a walk on the shingle, and I could walk there without drooping and wilting. We laughed a lot. I remember telling him how I'd moved old Parkes' bed into a draught and damped it down as though I was going to iron it, on the night before my wedding, just to encourage the lumbago and give Dickon a chance to get well in with Eloise.

We scrambled up the cliff again at a lower point and were walking home by the lane, when we saw a woman mounting the rise which had hidden her from us.

I hissed out, 'Mrs. Baker, where I lodged' and kind of dithered, not sure whether it was best to turn round or to walk on. Dickon took me by the arm and said, 'Keep calm. Slump over a bit, lean on me and don't say much.'

By that time Mrs. Baker judged that she was within hailing distance.

'Good afternoon, sir. Good afternoon, ma'am. I just been up to the house. There was a few little things the other poor lady left.'

'You mean Mrs. Meekin?'

'That's right. You remember when you come for her trunk I told you there was some stockings and things she'd asked me to rub out for her as soon as she arrived. I'd have brought them up afore, only my steady has been in bed with the 'flu. I tell him that's too early in the year for the 'flu. "If you're going to start now," I says to him, "you'll beat your own record." Six times last year he had it.'

'You shouldn't have troubled,' said Richard in his most kindly condescending manner. 'It's a long pull from the village.'

She took out a big white handkerchief and mopped her hot red face.

'It is that, sir. And if I'd of known that poor Mrs. Meekin intended to walk any part of the way I'd have warned her and she might have been here now. I said to old Lorkin, "You're a fool," I said, "ever to have let the lady get out there and walk, all in the dark too. Why didn't you tell her," I said, "that it was as much as your old motor can do to get up there?" Of course that's why he let her do it, he's that mortal afraid his old bumble bus'll break down, he dassent take her off the level.'

All the while she was talking—and I knew how she could talk, she was eyeing me. It might have been mere village curiosity and again it might not. I drooped over and hung on Richard's arm and tried to keep him between us, but I did really dread that I should suddenly see recognition break out over her face. And I was in this thing now. I was an accessory in the cheating; I'd let myself be buried. I pinched Richard's arm. He turned to me and said:

'Well, darling, I don't think you should be standing here. You've had quite a long walk today as it is.'

'Have you been ill, ma'am?'

'Not exactly,' I said, remembering to use my quiet Eloise voice. 'My little girl was ill in the spring and I rather overdid it nursing her. But your Broddy air is doing me a great deal of good.'

'Well, seeing you here give me right a turn. If it'd been dusk and the gentleman not here I'd have run all the way home screaming my head off. I'd have thought you was a ghost. So like the poor dead lady you are, if you'll excuse my saying so.' She gave a snicker of nervous laughter.

I tugged at Richard's arm, but I suppose he thought that this called for some explanation.

'There is quite a remarkable resemblance. Everyone notices it. My wife and Mrs. Meekin were cousins; and their mothers were twins.'

'Such a pretty lady, I thought, and so pleasant too,' she drooled on, digging her feet even firmer into the turf. 'A pleasure to do things for. And what a shock it must have been for you both. I'm sure you could have blown me over with a sneeze when I heard. I said to Baker, "Mark my words," I said, "there's . . ."'

I could think of only one thing to do. Dickon seemed

134

incapable of tearing himself away, so I took out my hand-kerchief and pretended to cry.

'My wife hasn't got over it yet,' he said. 'Come along, darling, you know you mustn't upset yourself. You'll make yourself ill. Good afternoon, Mrs. Baker. Thank you once more for bringing up the things.'

'I'm so sorry if I've upset the lady now.' She trotted after us like a dog, gasping out apologies. 'I wouldn't have for all the world. Baker always says my tongue runs away with me.'

'It's all right, really. Good-bye,' I mumbled through my handkerchief, and she finally took the hint, said good after-noon about four times over and trotted off along the lane.

'Let that be a lesson to you, and leave your sun worship till you're out of St. Brodric,' said Richard, stopping and letting go my arm while he lighted a cigarette. 'My God! That woman's tongue. I pity Baker, whoever he is.'

'Her eyes are worse than her tongue,' I said. 'She was simply devouring me.'

'That's why I thought it was worth taking a moment or two and explaining. If we'd just hurried past she'd have felt aggrieved and probably thought about it more than she will do now.'

'Quite a psychologist, aren't you? I always said you could have written a novel.

'In a way I have,' he returned complacently. 'Think what a story this would make, sympathetically handled of course.'

'Well, I hope to God nobody will ever have the handling of it. I've no yearnings to sample prison life. Come to that, if we could just get away from here and start having a little fun my present situation suits me very well. There is enough money to last us out, isn't there? Eloise hadn't been living on her capital or gambling or anything?'

'There's no evidence of anything of the kind. I suppose

if the money did suddenly go you'd go with it, you heartless hussy.'

'I don't know what I would do. I wake in the night sometimes and wonder. Next to being found out—in which case, of course, ways and means wouldn't trouble me for a season, we'd live at the Government's expense for once—but next to that I do dread suddenly finding the cash at an end.'

And I did. I knew how easily one drops out. I'd had that experience when I went back to London after being turned out of the Chimney House. And I couldn't face with any great joy the prospect of going back again. I wanted to be done with the Helpers' Club. (You know, a perfect lady of the bluest blood and impeccable references supplied for about a third of what they'd have to give a dirty little skivvy.) Done with Alex Lindon, who occasionally gave me a guinea for a photograph where I grinned delighted with a carpet sweeper or a new tooth-paste, or showed what a remarkable improvement some sort of girdle had made to my unfortunate figure. Done with racing out to Denham in the choicest portion of my well-stocked wardrobe, to stand in draughty passages all day and then be told I wasn't wanted. And the awful thing was that once before I had thought that I'd done with them. When I pranced up the aisle on Joshua's arm I thought that was all over for ever. A sort of mental Farewell to Arms. But it wasn't. And for a long time, as I had to work my way in again and remind heartless people of my existence, I had hated Joshua, silly gutless old fool. He'd made all that dough once and he could have done the same again; if he'd had any faith in his brain he needn't have burst it in despair. And after that little interlude I wasn't very easily lulled into a sense of security again. Something might happen, even now. And I used to think sometimes that though I had utterly refused Richard's love-in-a-corner-house kind of offer, that might be just what we were destined for. And that, of course, made me the more anxious to have a good time while it was to be had.

And I must admit frankly that living at Moat Place and mothering Diana and drooping about the house in Eloise's way was not my idea of having a good time. I'm domesticated in a sense because I have had to be, but it isn't my style of thing at all, and I loathe gardening. I like shops and theatres and amusing places in which to eat and drink. I like crowds of people and new clothes. So during the first weeks of October it seemed to me that, apart from having Richard for company and a semi-secure background, I wasn't much better off than I had been before. I had at least always had the excitement of the possibility of something happening and the stimulus of having somebody to please and manage. Dick was all too easily pleased and needed very little managing. I got to the state where it was quite exciting to be driven into Notham St. Mary and see a picture that was six months old.

Finally I said, 'Look here, Dickon, this is beginning to pall. How about a trip to town?' Like a lamb, he fell in with the suggestion and we had a fine old time. It was divine to be able to walk into any shop and buy anything. It was heaven, when I couldn't decide between two things, and the saleswoman, with the usual smirk, said, 'They both suit madam so well,' to be able to say, 'I'll have them both.' It was marvellous to go out night after night and think, 'Hang the expense,' and to know, from the glares of the women, that I hadn't lost my dress sense, and from the stares of the men that there was just something left at least of what I value far more.

We made several trips after that, though we never stayed very long. Richard had a kind of phobia about leaving the house with only the child, Miss Duffield and the servants in it. Some of them would be getting friendly with somebody in the village, he said. So back we'd go to St. Brodric to watch over our secret, rather like that man in the film who'd buried a fellow in his garden and then couldn't leave the spot again even to go to work.

'But soon, in the spring at the latest, we'll shut it up and go abroad,' he promised. So I waited with what patience I could muster.

I'm not sure that Dickon was as happy as he had expected to be. As a lover he was as good as ever, but now and again he'd look troubled and would sit or stand quite still with a far-away look in his eyes and if I spoke to him he would start and speak quite sharply. I guessed that the place was getting on his nerves too. I know it was on mine. The funny thing was that you never got used to it. It had a sinister feeling that grew, if anything, stronger with the passing of time. I caught myself getting nutty ideas about Eloise resenting my imposture and haunting me, not with groans or footsteps or the sound of chains dragging, but with an invisible and unfriendly presence. I shook them off as being ideas worthy of her herself, and yet that very comparison set me wondering whether by pretending to be another person you didn't tend to become like them.

One day, just before Christmas, I laughed and said to Dickon, 'I'm going to lay Eloise today. See this advertisement? Some mission wants some junk. I'm going to send the lot.'

So I emptied all her cupboards and drawers. I was literally amazed at the amount of stuff she had collected. Good tailored suits, hopelessly out of date, satin blouses, whole dozens of them, fur-plastered coats, shoes, dowdy hats. I bundled the lot together in two great parcels. I kept only one thing, and that was a little pink feather cape, an absolute poppet. The ostrich plumes curved out from the neck, over the shoulders, and just turned in at the elbows.

'God,' I said, holding it up, 'no slum woman would want this, would she? And really it is pretty. How on earth did Eloise come by such an adequate thing?'

'I gave it to her,' said Dick, 'and she always looked like a hen on the moult in it somehow. You put it on.'

I did so. It was absolutely wizard. I'd never seen anything so becoming as that soft, curling, fluttering pinkness.

'I dislike pink as a rule and I wanted to clear Eloise out of the house, but I'm not parting with this,' I said.

So I kept it round my shoulders while Dick kissed me and said one of his speeches. Then he corded up the bundles and took them down to the car to take them to the station and I finished clearing out the drawers. A few things, medicines and what not, I put in their proper place in the bathroom cabinet, thinking how like Eloise it was to keep her pills all muddled in with her powder, and the rest I flung away.

I felt so much better after that, whether it was the effort or the effect of the clearance, that I was able to really make plans for the New Year. Dickon agreed that Diana should go to school and we'd go abroad. We were going to the South of France, and with the thought of sun and mimosa and merry doings already mellowing my mind I determined that everyone should have a happy Christmas.

Partly perhaps I did it out of conscience. I was sending Diana off to school as though she were an orphan and I was casting Miss Duffield back to the Helpers' when no doubt she had thought that she was comfortably dug in for several years. So I tried to make up for it by buying them both extravagant presents. And having really got into the spirit of the thing, I even included Emma Plume, though in her case my conscience was crystal clear. I had come upon Diana laboriously stitching a pin-cushion, and Miss Duffield painting, with no little skill, a portrait of the child, and was told that they were both to be presents to Nanny. So from force of habit almost I asked myself, 'What would Eloise do?' and decided that not only would she have sent the old girl a present herself, she would have persuaded Dickon to do the same. And though, in malice, Dickon chose a present that was bound to annoy, I gave fifteen bob for a gift that I thought couldn't fail to please even Emma Plume. And as I packed it I thought of the times the hag had been spiteful and unfair to me as a child and suspicious and unfriendly to me later on. I was astonished at my own magnanimity.

But then, God love us, it isn't hard to be magnanimous when you're on top of the world yourself. And as soon as we had really decided to leave Moat Place that's where Dickon and I were. And we were never coming back, that we had decided. We were going to play about in the sun for a time and then go round the world, see everything, do everything. I'd so often thought, 'If only I had Eloise's money wouldn't I make it fly!' And now I had it, and that thought eased me rather, because it wasn't as if she'd ever enjoyed herself properly, poor devil. If she hadn't yelped herself into a heart attack she'd have moped into a decline or put herself out, like Aunt Ella. I'd never seen her on top of the world simply because she was alive and had some money.

So for about the thousandth time I pushed Eloise out of my mind and we prepared for a grand Christmas with all the little traditional bits: fancy tins of tea for all the old women, tobacco for the old men and toys for all the kids that we knew by sight.

Miss Duffield mucked it up a bit at the very end. On the day before Christmas Eve, in the evening, she got a telephone call and came back into the room where we were dressing the most marvellous tree for Diana, looking a bit queer. She didn't say anything that might lead us to think that she'd had bad news, but she seemed rather quiet and we thought perhaps somebody with whom she'd once had good times had just rung her up to wish her a happy Christmas or something. So Dickon, who always took a good view of Miss Duffield—in which I shared—soon got out the bottles and began to mix a noggin, thinking to cheer her up. But she went off to bed, still queer and quiet, and in the morning she came down dressed for travelling and said that she must go.

We tried to get out of her what the matter was; because it must have been something pretty sudden, considering that she had seemed delighted with the idea of spending Christmas with her dear Diana, and we'd even arranged that she should stay on and take the child to Melwood on the first day of the term. We were making it worth her while, too. Because honestly I'd rather have gone without a new frock, if that were necessary, than be left to cope with that child who never, by any chance, did anything I asked her to. But though we pried and questioned, Miss Duffield was adamant. She wouldn't tell us anything; and yet all the while she seemed to be wanting to say something, sort of half opening her mouth and then shutting it again. And at the very end, when Dickon had got the car out to take her to the station, she turned round and stood on one foot and said quite sharply, 'Mrs. Curwen . . .'

'Well,' I said, thinking that it was coming at last, especially as she was looking at me in an eager kind of way, and with a gleam of affection, too. But her face shut down again, and she said lamely:

'Good-bye. I hope you'll have a happy Christmas and enjoy your trip.'

'I'd have a happier Christmas if you would let us cope with whatever is bothering you and see if we couldn't persuade you to stay,' I said frankly.

'I don't think you would,' she said with a peculiar smile. 'And I don't think Diana will be troublesome. She promised to be good. I'm sorry to go like this, but you know what relatives are. . . .'

She climbed into the car and Dickon started the engine.

'Don't forget the list of things I gave you,' I called to him.

I dived back indoors into the warm and tried to forget Miss Duffield, who had, I felt, let us down. I had gone to the telephone last evening when it rang and now I tried to remember whether the voice of the person who asked for Miss Duffield had sounded agitated. I hadn't taken much notice, and I couldn't really remember. And then it shot through my brain that the voice had been *like* one I knew, a prim, countrified voice. . . . Suddenly I knew. It was a voice like Emma Plume's, with its subdued Midland accent.

It couldn't have been hers, of course. She would not have asked for Miss Duffield, whom she had never met. But the likeness interested me now I had traced it, and I meant to mention it to Dickon. But it completely escaped my mind.

Emma Plume

I soon found myself a new job, not the one with the twins, but a very nice one with a lady in Dersingham Gardens, Kensington. There was only one child, a little boy, just four years old, nice enough, but not to be compared with my Miss Diana. I missed her every day, and doing all the things which a nurse must do for a child only served to remind me.

As soon as I was settled I wrote to Miss Duffield, pretending that it was just to give her my address, but really in the hope that she would write to me. No letter came, however, for several weeks, and when it did I pounced on it like a starving man would pounce on a beefsteak pudding.

Dear Miss Plume,

I have been meaning to answer your letter for several days now, but there has been such a lot to do. You know how it is when you begin putting off things till tomorrow. But Mrs. Curwen has taken the child on to the beach for a while and I am free at last.

Well, I suppose that really you are panting for news. I have very little really. Apparently just before our arrival there was a little commotion. Mrs. Meekin, Mrs. Curwen's cousin, was coming up here to dinner one night and died of heart failure, either just outside or just inside the house, I am not sure which. She was buried in the churchyard here. You may remember the lady. I dare say it was a shock for Mrs. Curwen, but she seems to have got over it, and is far less of an invalid than you had led me to believe.

I get on quite well with Diana. She is quite bright and intelligent though not inclined to concentrate. I mind everything you told me about keeping her warm and her feet dry and I promise you that I don't work her too hard. If she were here I would try to get her to write a line or two to you. She is beginning to make quite firm distinct letters.

All the servants seem to be new. No one remembers you.

Perhaps I ought to tell you that when it was discovered that you were not returning there was a great uproar. I was surprised at the temper shown by so young a child. She threw herself on the floor and screamed and kicked. Kind treatment having failed, Mrs. Curwen was driven to force and slapped her—only once, I will add for your comfort.

Oh, and the donkey was a great surprise. Nobody seemed to know anything about it. However, it arrived quite safely and is now grazing by the side of what is known as the lane, a stretch of grass studded with gorse.

Well, I think that is all the news, and a poor lot I am sure you will think. I will write again and should be glad to hear from you. I hope you are well and happy.

Yours sincerely,
Myra Duffield.

I pored over that letter quite a lot. The part about Miss Antonia puzzled me. I was sorry that she should be dead, so young, too, though I had never liked her when she was a child, and of course, after the way she had carried on with Miss Eloise's husband, I never thought well of her. She always had been a fast, painted hussy. I was surprised to hear that she had ever been invited to the new house, even for dinner. But then, Miss Eloise was always so soft-hearted, she would forgive her worst enemy, and that Miss Antonia was. Though you shouldn't ever think ill of the dead.

I was a little hurt, too, that Miss Eloise hadn't written to me herself. I somehow expected that she would. I know that she was exhausted after the move and probably had a lot to do in the new house. But Miss Duffield spoke as though she was in pretty good health again and able to walk quite a bit. Still, I was glad of that, and it would do her more good to be out in the air than stuffing in, writing letters to me. I was sorry though that Miss Diana had got herself smacked over me. Poor little dear, she had a faithful heart.

I folded the letter away with a sigh. But even after it was hidden between my best gloves and the handkerchiefs that Miss Diana had given me for my birthday, I still seemed to see phrases from it, written across the things I looked at. And those phrases seemed to be trying to tell me something; as though, written between the words that could be seen, there were others which were meant for me to read if only I had a special kind of sight. It worried me quite a bit, for I didn't like to think that I was getting fanciful in my old age, not that I was so old. But I'd never known Miss Eloise to smack anything—not even her dolls —and the thought of smacking Miss Diana was like the things you dream about, quite possible by all ordinary reckonings and yet most unlikely. And the donkey, too. She must have known that there was some likelihood of its arrival, after my letter and that telegram.

I had to make quite an effort to keep my mind on my work and to do my duty as I liked to do it. Once or twice

I found myself quite snappish when young Master Cedric did something to draw my mind from my thoughts; and I took myself to task, saying, 'Emma Plume, your duty is here and you must give your mind to it.'

Nevertheless I answered Miss Duffield's letter very promptly and waited with a good deal of impatience to hear from her again.

The weeks followed one another very quickly and soon we were thinking about Christmas. I bought a doll in one of the stores and made it a complete outfit which would take on and off. That was for Miss Diana. For Miss Eloise I knitted an angora bed-jacket of palest shell pink brushed up round the neck and the edges of the little sleeves until it looked almost as though it was edged with swansdown.

I posted these early because the new family were going down to Devon for the holiday and I was going with them. I didn't know how the posts would be from there and anyway I didn't want to have to pack the things twice. I also sent a calendar for Miss Duffield, a very pretty tear-off one with a motto for every day of the year and a bowl of anemones on it.

I heard from Moat Place on the day before we started for Devon and put the package and the letters away until evening when all the packing was done and Master Cedric asleep.

I opened each thing slowly, savouring it. From Miss Duffield there was a present which proved that I was right in thinking well of her. She couldn't have sent me anything I would have valued more if she had spent pounds on it. It was a little water-colour sketch of Miss Diana and it was very well done indeed. There were the yellow curls that I'd always taken such pleasure in tending, the sweet little pink and white face, the blue eyes and dear little neck. It faded away at the neckline of the dress, just coloured enough for me to recognise the blue silk dress which was one of the last things I had knitted her. It was glazed and framed in white wood and was, apart from the memories it called up, a very pretty and decorative piece. I kissed the cold glass before setting it on my dressing-table. I thought, 'I'll show it to Mrs. Forsdyke in the morning. I've often told her how sweet my last child was, now she can see for herself that I wasn't exaggerating.'

Miss Diana had sent me a pin-cushion made of white flannel in the shape of a donkey. The saddle was of red silk and had all kinds of pins in it. There was a note with it. I hadn't stopped to read Miss Duffield's letter because I was really looking for a letter or a word from Miss Eloise, but I had to stop to read the child's. She had printed it herself, bless her heart, on a piece of paper that had been ruled and then had the lines rubbed out.

Dear Nanny,
   This is Snowball. I sewed him and Miss Duffield cut him out. He is full of sawdust. I hope you will like him. I wish you were here. I hope you will have a happy Christmas and come to see me in the New Year. With lots of love from Diana.

Next there was a book, brand new in a bright cover. It was called *Vitamins in the Nursery* and I knew at once that Mr. Curwen had sent that. It was just like him. He knew that I didn't want a present from him and he knew that I didn't believe all that kind of rubbish. Any woman with any sense knows that suet pudding and carrots are good for children without having them called Vitamin A or B. I put that aside quite quickly.

The last thing in the parcel was a flat soft package wrapped in tissue paper. I opened it and shook out a scarf. It was a good one, silk, blue and white in stripes; and I looked at it as though it had been a snake. Whatever had induced Miss Eloise to make fun of me in that way, at Christmas time, too! She knew that I never, in any weather, wore a scarf. I don't believe in them. When I was a child I had glands in my neck that used to swell and ache every winter. My mother, who was old-fashioned, used to tie flannel round my neck and never let me go out without a scarf up to my ears. And then, one day, we had a new doctor and he stripped it all off and said, 'Don't coddle a throat like that. Let it get the air to it and harden it off,' and we did and I never had a bad throat again from that time to this. I wouldn't wear a scarf for any money. Many and many's the time that Miss Eloise has said, 'Oh, Nanny, you look so cold. That mackintosh collar looks so chilly against your neck. Why don't you wear a scarf?' And I've always said, 'No scarves for me.' And now, for Christmas, she had sent me one. And no letter. There was a card with the scarf, a pretty one of snow and holly and a robin on it, the very picture of Christmas, and written inside, under the printed message of goodwill, there was, in Miss Eloise's writing, 'With love and best wishes to Nanny.'

'Oh well,' I thought, 'I expect she has worn herself out again and had to go to bed. Perhaps she got Miss Duffield to do the shopping for her and never even knew what she had chosen for me. It may not be carelessness or forgetfulness.'

I reached out for the letter that I had missed.

Dear Miss Plume,

As usual I must begin with apologies for delay in writing. I have been very busy, as you shall hear. I hope that you like the sketch of Diana. I did it myself, but I fully realise that I have only a little talent, and just a slight knack for catching a resemblance. She was very good about sitting still while I did it when she heard it was for you. If I had a jealous nature I'm afraid I should often find things to resent in her constant reference and unfailing devotion to you. N.B. I don't.

I told you that I had been busy. It has suddenly been decided to send Diana to Melwood, you know that super-posh boarding school for tinies. And as I thought that she was just a little backward for her age I have been working very hard so that she may not find things too difficult when she gets there. I happen to know that most of the children there are the offspring of people living abroad, India and China mostly, and they, for some reason, are always extremely precocious and I thought she might hate it if she found the others ahead of her. Added to this, there has been the getting of things ready as she is to go after Christmas, not to mention the correspondence connected with finding myself another post at such short notice.

I am rather sorry about it all, especially as it is, to a degree, the child's own fault. With me she behaves perfectly, but Mrs. Curwen seems absolutely helpless with her. I can't think why, but I must admit that I have seen her, with my own eyes, behave in such a completely disobedient and unruly manner when with her parents that it is difficult to believe that she is the same child as the little angel of the schoolroom. For Mrs. Curwen to express a wish is enough to make Diana run counter to it immediately.

Since she is always perfectly amenable with me you may imagine that I have had uncomfortable moments, especially as this queer mood seems to have coincided with my arrival. Some people would think that I had turned the child against her mother, but the Curwens have never suggested such a thing and when I mentioned it myself told me that the idea had never occurred to them.

Even so, perhaps, they would not have decided to send her to school quite so soon but they are anxious to go abroad early in the New Year. Mrs. Curwen appears to dislike the house and to regret having come to a spot so lonely and remote. And, of course, if she expresses a wish to him it is as good as fulfilled at once. I have been in several families and never seen a couple so much attached to one another. With all one reads of divorce in papers and novels and of the feeling that affection between married couples is old-fashioned, it does one good to meet a pair so entirely devoted.

All the same, although she dislikes the place, I think it has done her good. She is quite a different woman from the one you described to me that night at Hunstanton, far more easy to get on with, if I may say so.

I was glad to have your letter, though by the way I neglected to answer it you will hardly believe that. I hope that you will have a very happy Christmas and good fortune, health and happiness throughout the coming year. I will let you know when I get a new job. It might be somewhere near enough to you to allow us to meet occasionally for a cup of tea. I should like that.

Yours sincerely,
Myra Duffield.

I read the letter to the end, turned back and read every word again and then stood there with it drooping from my hand as though it had exploded and killed me where I stood.

Miss Diana not getting on with her mother.

Miss Eloise sending that delicate, precious child to a school meant for children who were as good as orphaned.

That scarf.

'She is quite a different woman.'

'A pair so entirely devoted.'

The donkey business.

My sudden dismissal.

They all fitted in like the pieces of a jigsaw puzzle, with

this difference. When the pieces fit in a puzzle you can see what they have combined to make. These pieces all fitted, but they made nonsense.

I took off the white apron which I had not bothered to remove since bathing my charge and went down to the drawing-room. Mrs. Forsdyke was on the hearth on her knees tying up parcels with coloured paper and silver twine. She looked up and said, 'Oh, come in, Nanny. Is everything ready?' I said, 'I'm very sorry, Mrs. Forsdyke, to have to say this at such a time, but I have news that compels me to go away. I can't go to Devon with you tomorrow.'

'Nonsense, Nanny, of course you must. Where could we find a nurse on the day before Christmas Eve? You poor thing, you're all upset. There, sit down and tell me all about it. We can think of some way to settle whatever it is, I'm sure, without your having to go anywhere.'

She swept a heap of little boxes off the settee and plumped up a cushion which she patted invitingly.

'I'm sorry,' I said. 'There's something that only I can do, and I must do it at once.'

'Surely,' she said, her voice hardening, 'it can wait until after Christmas. It simply must. I can't go to spend Christmas in Devon and have Cedric on my hands all the time. Just until after Christmas, Nanny.'

'No. I've waited too long already. I'm really more sorry than I can say about giving you such inconvenience, but it really is urgent. I must leave here tomorrow morning.'

Annoyance and curiosity struggled in her face.

'But what can it be? Is somebody ill—or dead?'

'That's what I have to find out, madam.'

'Well,' she said furiously, 'I must say, I've never heard of such a thing in all my days. A moment's notice, all our plans upset, and not a word of explanation. I should never have expected it of you. I thought you had *some* idea of loyalty and responsibility.'

'I have,' I said. 'But this is an older loyalty and a greater responsibility. I'm very sorry, but I must go.'

And after all, I thought, Christmas is supposed to be the children's festival; it wasn't so outrageous to think that she and his father would have to care for the child for just a few days. Or at least it didn't seem so to me at that moment.

I packed overnight and caught a train at ten o'clock from Liverpool Street. I'd tried to find out the easiest and quickest way to St. Brodric, but the booking office was crowded with people, all in holiday mood, laden with parcels and trailing children by the hand, and I could get no satisfactory answer from the clerk beyond the information that I must go to Colchester first.

The train was packed, and slow, and it was almost twelve before it reached Colchester. There I learned that I must go to Saxmundham, change there and go on a small branch line to Notham St. Mary, which was the nearest the train went to St. Brodric. The cross-country journey by slow train took me the whole of the afternoon and by the time I had reached Notham it was quite dark and very cold. I was cheered to find, however, that what was known as the station taxi made regular trips over the six miles between Notham and St. Brodric.

The driver of this vehicle, an old man huddled in an overcoat with many collars, was not disposed to leave the station at once. I said that I was in a hurry and offered him extra payment if he would start at once. He cleared his throat and spat.

'Sorry, lady,' he said, 'this here motorcar is called station taxi, and station taxi it be. I collect folkses here for St. Broddy and all the other villages and here I stay till the Ipswich train be in. 'Tain't so much the money as the reputation. If somebody get out of the Ipswich train and want to go to Ilborough, it ain't no comfort to he to know as you have paid me double, see?'

So after ascertaining that there was no other means of reaching my destination I climbed into the ancient vehicle and waited. Presently the Ipswich train arrived and two other passengers joined me. One was for Ilborough, the other for Welstead Green, which took us another four miles out of our way. If I had known my way, and if it had not been so dark, I should have alighted and walked, for by this time my impatience, my uncertainty and that underlying suspicion were driving me crazy.

But at last the old man and I were alone. He asked me over his shoulder what part of St. Brodric I wanted.

'There be Brodric Street and Brodric Bridge, you see. For Bridge you turn off soon. Wasted a lot of time and petrol I have, taking folkses to Broddy Street and they wanting Bridge all the time.'

'I don't know,' I said. 'I want to go to a house called Moat Place, perhaps you know it.'

'Should say I do,' he retorted. 'Why, the last time I went up there I had what was to be a corpsy in the back there. Dead within ten minutes she was.'

'Oh,' I said, not immediately interested.

'Ah, poor lady, that was very sad. In the midst of life we are in death. Would you believe it, she come to me as bright and pretty as could be and she say, "Will you take me up to Moat Place," she say, "I'm going up to dinner with my cousin and her husband and their car ain't working and I can't walk that far." So I take her and when we get to the gate off the lane she say, "I'll get out here. It'll do me good to get some air," she say. And she walk up and get there dead. Very weak heart, you see, she had, and 'twas mostly uphill.'

I made an effort not to let my eagerness show in my

voice, for there is no more certain way than that of drying up gossip. 'What was the lady's name?'

'I might not have remembered that, but that she's laid in the churchyard bang next to my Agnes. Antonia Emelina Fryer Meekin is the full of it. Aged thirty-two years. Rest in Peace.'

'Very sad,' I said. 'I expect the cousins were very upset.'

'Maybe they were. I couldn't say. You know the family?'

'Very well,' I answered.

'Mr. Curwen now, he's a very nice gentleman, very friendly like. Not above calling in at the local and having a pint and standing one. Mrs. Curwen, we don't see much of, only as she go by in the car like.'

'She's very delicate.'

'Well, it's to be hoped she don't pop off like her poor cousin. See, there, that gate was where I dropped her and this what we're now going up in a second was what she walked up, with a heart like that and all.' He fiddled with his driving things and encouraged the car as though it were a horse. 'Come on now, Mary, just another pull. There, you've done it, good old girl.' Then he said, addressing me, 'See, there's the lights down below.'

'Then stop here, please. I want to give them a surprise.'

'Maybe that's what the other lady did. But you've gotten more sense than that one, you've only downhill to go. Ah, thank you kindly. Good night and a happy Christmas.'

I called back absently, 'Happy Christmas,' and started to walk between the bushes over the short damp turf towards the house.

On either side of the door there were three windows, all lighted, but as I approached those on the left went out, and instead the fan-light over the door sprang into sight. The windows on the right were not curtained. As I drew nearer

156

I could see figures moving about inside. I sheered off to the right so that I came close to the side of the house and stood near the blank wall beyond the yellow light thrown from the last window. I was so excited that my heart was thumping unevenly and I needed to stand still and to get my breath and to decide what to do.

I could, now that I was so near a solution, face the thought that had been holding me in terror all day. It had occurred to me, foolish as it may sound, that Miss Eloise was being held in that house, shut away, frightened, maybe ill-used. And perhaps, I thought, the woman whom Miss Duffield knows as Mrs. Curwen is not my Mrs. Curwen at all. I hadn't really *believed* that, because it was so far-fetched, like those silly stories, *A Prisoner in Her Cousin's House*, and so on, that Woods was always reading back at Chimney House. Also, I hadn't wanted to believe it. And yet it would explain all the things that had puzzled me, the child's behaviour, the scarf, Miss Duffield's words, 'A different woman.'

Well, I should soon know. I crept close to the wall and peered round the frame of the window and the curtain which hung, undrawn, just inside. The room was brightly lighted and there was a great log fire leaping up the chimney. On a table to the right of the fireplace there stood a Christmas tree, half decorated. Mr. Curwen was standing on some steps, twisting silver icicles amongst the boughs. He was talking to somebody, I could see his lips move, but the window fitted well and I could not hear what he said. The only sound that came to me was the sad wash and moan of the sea, which must have been very near the house.

Presently I saw Miss Duffield move into the part of the room which was within my vision, and she handed up some parcels to Mr. Curwen. He said something to her and she

157

laughed. He studied one parcel and then made a pretence of opening it. She reached up, snatched it away and put it behind her back, retreating out of reach.

And then a second woman came into sight. Miss Eloise.

I only saw her back, and I recognised the little pink feather cape which she was accustomed to wear over her thin dinner dresses. She stole the parcel from Miss Duffield and went forward to the tree, intending to hang it up herself. All this time she had her back to me. She fixed the parcel and turned. And as she did so a loud cry escaped me. For the woman in the pink feather cape was the woman who was supposed to be buried in the churchyard.

And if Miss Antonia was here, where was Miss Eloise? And who was it who lay under that headstone?

Fear, stark fear such as I had never known in my life, poured over me like cold water from a bucket. For a moment I feared that I was about to faint, a thing I have never done. But I was kept conscious, upright and alert by the fact that my cry had been heard. All three of them turned towards the window. Mr. Curwen jumped down from the ladder, crossed the room quickly and threw open the french window, the one next which I was standing, and first looked, then stepped out.

I had cowered back into the shelter of a bare winter jasmine bush and stood there, not breathing, rigid. He was so close that I could have touched him and I was terrified lest the heavy thumping of my heart should betray me. He looked to right and left, stepped out and looked in the shadow of the doorway and then returned to the window.

'It's nothing,' he called. 'A gull, I should think. I've heard them cry like that.'

He closed the window and drew the curtain over it. The other windows darkened one by one and I was alone in the night.

I tiptoed away from the house and regained the grass of the lane. It was very dark and there was no roadway to guide me. I ran into prickly bushes that tore my clothes and scratched my legs and twice I caught my foot in rabbit holes and fell face downward in the cold grass. But at last, after what seemed a long time, I came to the gateway which marked the end of the private ground and now there was the gritty road under my feet and I could tell when I strayed. At length that lane came out on the main road and by remembering that the car had turned left I was enabled to turn right and after another long, long spell of walking I saw the lights and roofs of the village.

The Post Office, which I found with some difficulty, for it was in a cottage, up a long garden, with only a little board to announce its purpose, was closed, shuttered and quite silent. I knocked twice and received no answer. Then I thought of the public-house. That would be open until ten o'clock. I walked on. Nobody seemed to be about. There were lights in some upper windows and here and there in a lower one. From some house too there came the sounds of a broadcast carol service.

I found the public-house at last and pushed open the door. Inside there was a thick fog of tobacco and human breath and a strong smell of shag and beer. My appearance seemed to arouse a good deal of interest; the buzz of conversation ceased and all eyes were turned toward me as I pushed my way to the bar, where a small man in shirt-sleeves released the handle of his beer machine, pushed over the glass he had just filled and then said, 'And what for you, Ma'am?'

'Have you a telephone?' I asked.

'Yeah. Through at the back. Addy, Addy, show the lady where the telly is, will you?'

A door at the back opened and a woman with very frizzy hair poked out her head and inquisitive face. The man lifted the flap of the counter and let me through. Behind me the buzz of conversation rose again.

Addy led me along a passage to a spot where it widened and held a bracket in the wall upon which stood a telephone.

'Could you tell me the number of Moat Place?' I asked her.

'Brodric one four,' she said. 'It'll take a bit of time to get through because our calls have to go to Notham.'

'Thank you,' I said, in what I hoped was a tone of dismissal. I didn't want her standing over me while I made the call. But she hung about and I was much exercised in my mind as to how I could express myself without letting her know too much. However, just as the voice at the other end said 'Hullo,' the call 'Addy! Addy!' was repeated and she was obliged, reluctantly, to tear herself away.

'Moat House?' I asked.

'Yes. Whom do you want?'

'Miss Duffield.'

'Hang on. I'll fetch her.'

After a moment or two, during which I dreaded that Addy would return, I heard Miss Duffield's high bright voice.

'Hullo,' she said. 'Who is it?'

'Emma Plume,' I said. 'Miss Duffield, this is frightfully important. Are you alone?'

'Why, yes. What is the matter? Where are you?'

'Never mind that. Listen. This may all sound very absurd to you, but can you tell me exactly what people are in the house at this minute?'

'Of course. Mr. and Mrs. Curwen. Four maids, myself and the child. Why?'

'Are you sure, can you swear that there isn't any other woman, perhaps locked away somewhere? Have you been in every room in the house?'

I heard her laugh. 'Of course I have. Miss Plume, you haven't been celebrating the season rather early, have you?'

'I have just discovered the most horrible and mysterious thing that I have ever been in contact with. You are quite *positive* that there is no one hidden in the house?'

'Positive.'

'All right,' I said, 'thank you. Please don't mention that I telephoned you. As you have any respect for justice and the law of the land, promise me that.'

'All right.' Her voice was puzzled and dubious and I was dismally sure that she thought me either drunk or mad.

I hung up the receiver. It was just closing time and the whole house seemed to shake with the noise of heavy boots, the repeated slamming of the door, the loud, jocular good nights. I stood in the narrow passage trying to collect my thoughts and make a plan of action. I had no experience to go upon; no one to consult. What was to be done I must do alone.

Addy returned from the bar.

'I wonder,' I began, 'whether you could put me up for the night. All my plans have gone wrong and I shall have to stay in the village until tomorrow. Any kind of bed would do.'

'We've a perfectly good spare room,' she replied with some sharpness. 'I'll just need to put sheets on the bed. It is aired.'

'Thank you,' I said. 'It's just ten o'clock, isn't it? I think I might just catch the doctor. Where does he live?'

She looked at me unfavourably. 'Are you ill? Because if you are I don't think we can lodge you. With Christmas coming, just our busiest time, we don't want sickness in the house.'

'I'm perfectly all right. Where does the doctor live?'

'Just along the street. Turn left when you go out and

it's a big square white house with railings in front of it. You can't miss it.'

'And his name is ——?'

'Adams.'

'Thank you. You can get the bed ready while I am gone.'

From the public-house to the doctor's was about seven minutes' walk, and in that seven minutes I did more hard thinking than I have ever done in the same amount of time before. My first thought, when I saw Miss Antonia there installed, was that Miss Eloise had been put away in the house somewhere, helpless, friendless and probably by this time half demented. I had read of such things. I knew that this didn't explain the presence of Miss Antonia's name on a headstone, but it might all be part of the trick. But Miss Duffield had said she was positive that there was no hiding-place in the house. And then it had burst upon me that it might be my Miss Eloise who was dead and buried. How that should be brought about I did not know, but if it had been it was my business to find out. I felt distracted, and I have no doubt I looked it, though I did pull on my gloves and straighten my hat before ringing the bell beside the wide white front door of the doctor's house. I was going on such a queer errand that I had only to look a bit foolish for him to conclude, as Miss Duffield had done, that I was crazy or intoxicated.

A neat parlourmaid opened the door to me and said that if I would wait a moment she would ask the doctor whether he would see me. So I stood just inside the door on the mat and fought for calmness and clearness of mind, though all the time my heart and all my other organs seemed to be shaking and quivering like a badly set jelly.

After a short delay the doctor, an old man, with a pipe in his hand and carpet slippers on his feet, came shuffling through a door, opened another and said, 'Come in here, will you?' He switched on a light and knelt down to plug in an electric heater which stood in the empty hearth.

'Now,' he said, straightening himself, 'what can I do for you?'

'I don't quite know,' I said. 'I want to ask you some questions.'

'Then we'd better both sit down, hadn't we? You take that chair. That's right. Dear me, you look rather upset. There, take your time and then tell me all about it.'

'A little while ago, in September, I think, or early October, a Mrs. Meekin went up to Moat Place one evening and died suddenly. I suppose they called you in, didn't they?'

'They did indeed. Yes, yes, I remember quite well. Mr. Curwen sent for me and I went up immediately. Unfortunately there was nothing I could do, the poor woman was quite dead.'

'Had you ever seen her before?'

'Yes. She had come in to see me a couple of days before. She appeared to be a little nervous about her heart—rather unnecessarily, so I thought at the time. Events proved me wrong.'

'And have you ever seen Mrs. Curwen?'

'No, never. I am not socially inclined and have no wife to make those contacts for me. And although I have heard that Mrs. Curwen does not enjoy very good health she has never apparently thought of asking my advice for its improvement. And now, my dear lady, may I ask what is the point in all these questions?'

'Just one more, please. Believe me, I am not asking them for the sake of asking. I have a very real, very grave reason for what looks like my curiosity. Would you, could you, tell me what kind of woman Mrs. Meekin was—what she looked like, both times you saw her?'

'When she came to see me she impressed me very much. She was pretty and had a bright manner. She was round about thirty years old. Her hair was auburn and I remember thinking how nice it was to see a woman with a proper head of hair.'

'And the dead woman?'

'Very much the same, of course. She had only been dead an hour. Really, I fail to see where these slightly morbid questions are leading.'

'To this. Are you quite certain, certain beyond all doubt, that the woman who came to see you and the woman whom you were called to see was the same person?'

He stared at me, his pipe suspended from his hand and his lower lip falling.

'What are you suggesting?' he asked at last. 'Of course I'm sure. I had never seen Mrs. Meekin without a hat before and there was, naturally, a lack of expression and a pallor about the dead face . . . but it was the same woman.'

'Think carefully,' I said. 'A matter of the most serious importance may hang upon your answer. Could you swear, in a court of law if necessary, that your patient of the morning was the corpse of the evening? Not somebody like her, but the same?'

He stood up as quickly as his age would allow and looked down at me. 'Madam,' he spluttered, 'I demand an explanation. You arrive, without appointment, at a late hour. You ask me several questions, without authority, and then you appear to doubt my word and mention courts of law. What is your connection with the dead woman and what, in the name of goodness, are you trying to insinuate?'

'Don't be angry,' I said. 'I'm not insinuating anything. I am trying to find out why Mrs. Meekin, who is supposedly buried, is up at Moat Place at this moment masquerading as Mrs. Curwen.'

He sat down again, more suddenly than he had risen.

'Are you sure? Do you realise the significance of what you are saying?'

'Only too well.'

'Who are you? A relation?'

'I was nurse to Mrs. Curwen's little girl. I am prepared to prove the truth of what I am saying. But you will understand that if what I fear and dread has happened is really the case this is a tricky business to move in. We have to be quite certain of every step before we take it. Now, in the light of what I have told you, will you think back and try to remember any differences, however slight, that you may have noticed, or thought you noticed, between the two women you examined?'

He was silent for so long that I had given up all hope of any fact forthcoming. Then suddenly he leaned forward.

'Just one thing, very small. I did remark to Mr. Curwen that if I had realised that Mrs. Meekin was so very thin I would have given her a few words of advice about diet.'

'That's not a small thing,' I said. 'Miss Eloise was always the slighter of the two. She took life harder and that sort never make flesh. So she's dead. And buried in Miss Antonia's name. Now why?' And then suddenly it was my turn to remember something, to lean forward as he had done and confide what I had remembered. 'The money,' I said, 'that blasted money. It never did her any good and it brought her to her end.'

'To her end, you say? Oh no, oh no. There you overreach yourself. If you are implying that the corpse was indeed that of the real Mrs. Curwen, I can assure you that she was not "brought to her end." Her death was as natural as I hope our own will be, and less painful than we dare hope for. It is just remotely possible that I was mistaken as to identity, but as to cause of death, no. She died of heart failure.'

'And what made her heart fail? Can you answer that? He probably upset her, staged a quarrel, had another love affair with somebody. There were a thousand things he might have done. But we can leave that. That is a matter for the police.'

'Now I must warn you,' he said, 'before you begin to call in the police you must be very sure of your ground. If your surmise is true you are up against a clever trick, well planned and well executed. You may not be able to *prove* that the lady at Moat Place is not indeed Mrs. Curwen. Have you thought of that? My remark that I had not noticed how thin the deceased was may have seemed significant to you, but it won't go far, not with the police anyway. Even to me it means little, I almost wonder at myself for noticing or mentioning it. What other evidence could you bring—supposing the unfortunate lady were to be exhumed, shall we say?'

'Miss Eloise had had three teeth extracted. When she was thirteen her teeth were growing crooked because they were overcrowded in the top jaw. She had two out, one on either side. And much later on, just before Miss Diana was born, she lost another. That was at the bottom, on the left. And once, when we were staying in the country, we found a cat in a rabbit trap, one of those awful iron things I tried to stop her but she would try to let it out and the cat, poor thing, meaning no harm, bit her wrist. The scars were always there and I remember her father gave her a wide gold bracelet to wear over them. "A decoration for valour," he called it. And she had a little toe that was always bent, like that.' I showed him my crooked little finger. 'And although her hair was the same colour as her cousin's, it wasn't a bit like it. It was softer, not so wavy, and it was long, too, far longer than Miss Antonia's, for all she's grown hers so craftily.'

'Here,' he said, interrupting me. 'I'd better put those down. That would at least prove that you didn't imagine them or make them up afterwards.' He drew a small note book out of his pocket, screwed a silver pencil to a point and wrote, 'Three teeth, two top, one lower. Scar on wrist, crooked fourth toe, different hair.'

'And now what do you propose to do?' he asked. I had an answer ready for that. It had come to me when I mentioned money. 'I'm going to find the lawyer who made her father's will and has charge of her affairs. It's a firm with three names; two I forget, but one was Tickle. I shall always remember that because I thought it was a funny name to have. And I hope old Mr. Tickle is still alive even if he has retired. He knew my Miss Eloise as a child and in the good old Birmingham days he used to come to dinner three or four times a year. I shall go to Birmingham and find him.'

'Tomorrow is Christmas Eve and he may well be from home. Also, I doubt whether you would get to Birmingham from here before early on Christmas morning. There must be a better way than that. Now let me think. Birmingham, Birmingham. Ah yes, I have it. Dear me, my memory is very unreliable these days. I had a young locum here some time last year, and he subsequently went to Birmingham, bought a practice. I kept his name and address somewhere because I had to post several things on to him. I wonder, did I put it in my book?'

He shuffled to his desk, opened a drawer, the most untidy drawer I have ever seen, and stirred about amongst the papers, loose string, paper-fasteners and rubber-bands for a good five minutes. But he produced the book. Having done so, he rustled about in his memory again and said, 'It began with S. Of that I am sure. Now is it here? S. Savage, Sennet, now why did I ever put that name in here? Sinclair, poor chap, he's been dead for years. Sansom, Swann. Ah, here it is, Sloane, that's the fellow. And his telephone number too. Now if you'll excuse me I'll see if I can get in touch with Sloane and ask him if he knows a firm of solicitors with Tickle in it. You did say "Tickle," didn't you?

I'll just make a note of that. Meanwhile, and it may take some time, I'll get my good Flossie to bring you something hot. Would you like tea, or coffee, or maybe something a little stronger?'

'I don't want to bother anyone at this time of night. But tea is my drink.'

'So it is mine. And Flossie is used to my demands at any hour. This room is warmer now. Take off your coat and make yourself comfortable. I'll be back as soon as I can.'

I realised that though my new ally might be old and doddery and forgetful, he was willing and helpful and resourceful. I drank some tea and was grateful for it. And I shed a few tears when it came upon me, sitting there alone, that Miss Eloise had died, with me not there to ease her passing, and that that cold-blooded hound who never had loved her and that painted hussy who had wronged her had contrived between them to rob her even of her own name on the headstone.

In my mind anxiety had given way to certainty, and in the place of suspicion I now cherished a desire for vengeance, and a determination that I would have it.

The clock on the mantel chimed eleven and was answered by the whirring boom of the tall clock that I had noticed in the hall. Another quarter of an hour passed and then the old doctor shuffled back, triumph on his face and a slip of paper in his hand.

'Splendid fellow, Sloane. Excellent at research. He found the firm of Manson, Croome and Tickle in the telephone book and tracked down Mr. Wallace Tickle and rang him up to find out if he were the member of the firm of that name. Also, he ascertained that Mr. Tickle is intending to spend Christmas by his own hearth, wise fellow. All the telephone numbers and addresses are here. If I might suggest, I should think it would be as well if you rang him up and suggested meeting at a half-way house, or even that he came here. He'll be obliged to come here sooner or later. Now is there anything else I can do for you? Then perhaps we had better say good night. I expect we shall have occasion to meet again in this unhappy business. Try not to worry too much.'

'I can't thank you properly for all you have done. But I am grateful, indeed I am.'

I had some difficulty in getting back to my room; the house was locked up and in darkness. I knocked and knocked, and was at last admitted by the woman, who said disagreeably that they had given me up. The bed was extremely lumpy and the bedclothes, although very heavy, far from warm. I spent a miserable night, pondering the events of the day, imagining what might happen tomorrow, fretting for Miss Eloise, poor soul, and falling into short, unrefreshing little sleeps of exhaustion which only served to bring me dreams which woke me to think again.

I rose as soon as it began to be light and washed in the icy water from the jug. I held the cold sponge against my eyes and forehead, seeking refreshment that way. It seemed a long time before Addy came to inform me that breakfast was ready and I could feel that the day had really begun. I went downstairs and faced an unappetising meal of very fat bacon and stewed tea. Over it the woman inquired whether I should be staying any longer. I said I thought so and paid her for what I had already had. At last it was a quarter to nine and I went upstairs, deliberately not hurrying, put on my outer clothes and walked slowly to the Post Office, where I hoped that the telephone would not be in public passage. If it was I decided that I would go back to the doctor's house and beg him to add to his kindness by letting me use his. No inkling of my discovery must be allowed to escape and possibly warn the couple at Moat House; yet at the same time I must speak clearly and strongly enough to rouse Mr. Tickle's interest.

Fortunately the telephone at the Post Office was in a little red booth with a well-fitting door, and after finding what I wanted the post-mistress went back again to her breakfast, in which, from the state of her mouth, I judged that a very lightly cooked egg was included.

At about seven minutes past nine I was invited to place two shillings in the slot and in another minute I heard the voice that I remembered quite well as Mr. Tickle's.

I forced myself to speak clearly and slowly, though the thought that at last I was in touch with someone who would feel something of what I felt about the whole affair made me want to spill everything at once in a muddled rush.

'I'm sorry to disturb you on such a day and at such an hour,' I began. 'I am Emma Plume, for many years I was in the service of Miss Eloise Everard, of Merivale Avenue, Birmingham. You remember her?' His 'Yes indeed' came so faintly that I asked, almost in alarm, 'Can you hear me plainly?' The answer was rather stronger. 'Yes, quite well.'

'Then listen . . . and don't think that I am crazy. This is extremely important. I learned yesterday that she is dead, has been dead since the end of September, and her cousin —in whose name she was buried here—is taking her place as the wife of the man she married.'

There was a moment's silence, and then, 'I think you must be mistaken, you know. The Miss Everard whom I remember, she became Mrs. Curwen, and I heard from her only ten days ago. A business letter. And yesterday I received a Christmas greeting from her as well, just as usual.'

'You thought you did. I had one, too. Somebody can reproduce her writing very cleverly. But, Mr. Tickle, sir, you really must believe me. I have seen Mrs. Curwen at Moat

House, and she is not Miss Eloise. She is Miss Antonia, the cousin whom old Mr. Everard sent to school, you remember . . .' Here the wretched telephone interrupted me and, sweating, I had to fumble for another shilling, which rolled from my fingers and delayed me. 'Are you there? You see, I guess that Mr. Curwen and Miss Antonia cooked up this scheme because of the money—he couldn't touch it if Miss Eloise was dead, could he? Something must be done, and I thought you were the right person to do it. Please, please do something. It isn't just my imagination—the doctor has doubts too.'

'Where are you?'

'In the village, St. Brodric, where they are.'

'Of course, you realise that it is a serious charge that you are making. If it is indeed true it will be a matter for the police. False pretences and wrong information in registering a death. You are quite certain that you have not made a mistake?'

'I'm certain. I swear I am. I'm not satisfied about how Miss Eloise died, either. The doctor says he is certain it was heart failure, though. It may be that nothing can be proved. But whether he killed her or not, he's not going to live up there on her money, with that hussy, not while I am alive.'

'I think,' he said after a pause, 'that I ought to come along. It's a long journey at an awkward time of year and I am, as you know, no longer young. Still, this seems as if it should be looked into. Tell me, how does one get to St. Brodric?'

This time I had the shilling ready and the interruption lasted only a fraction of a second.

'It's awkward,' I admitted. 'You'll have to come to Colchester. Change and come on to Saxmundham. Change again for a place called Notham St. Mary. I'll see that you're met there.'

'Dear me. It could hardly be more involved, could it? I know what I'll do. My nephew is spending the holiday with me and he has a very fast car. I distrust it entirely but for once I think it may serve a good purpose. Three hundred and some odd miles, I suppose. Nearer four? Oh well. I imagine that we might be with you some time this afternoon. Where can I reach you?'

'At the public-house. There's only one. I'll be there. And bless you, sir, for believing me.'

'We may have cause to bless you—for your suspicions—again, of course, we may not. Well, I'll say good-bye for the present.'

I had all the hours of the morning and some of the afternoon to get through. I decided to go first and have a look at the grave. Not that it could tell me anything. There was a thick rim of frost over the grass and over the big shaggy white chrysanthemums which lifted their heads from a white marble vase that matched the headstone and the curb. It had only recently been set up, that headstone, I could see where the ground had been disturbed. The words on it were exactly those that the old man had quoted, 'Antonia Emelina Fryer Meekin. Aged thirty-two years. Rest in Peace.' The wickedness of it, and her up there as large as life playing about with parcels for a Christmas tree and laughing! I felt my eyes filling again. And once more, just as it had come upon me last night when the doctor had described the dead woman and I knew that Miss Eloise was indeed dead, it came upon me that *he* had had something to do with it. We might never be able to prove that, though not a stone should remain unturned; but at least he should not enjoy the fruits of his ill-doing.

As I turned sadly away I determined to find out, if I could, where and for how long Miss Antonia had stayed in the village before the fatal evening.

Fortune, or merely the fact that the sudden death had

been the most stirring thing in St. Brodric that autumn, favoured me. As I stepped over the frosty grass on to the gravel again an old man with a spade over his shoulder came around the corner of the church. He eyed me with some curiosity and said, 'Good morning. Seasonable weather.'

'Very,' I said, and lingered a little.

'Looking at the new stone, wuz you? Poor lady, she was took very sudden.'

'Did you know her?'

'Not to say know. But she wuz lodging with my niece, up at Myrtle Cottage. Right upset her that did. Bright pleasant lady she said she wuz. One of the nicest people she'd ever had and she should know. Bin taking in people for the best part of thirty year. Still them's the sort that allust go first, in my reckoning.'

The remark showed his own low opinion of his own brightness and pleasantness, for he was every day of eighty. He said 'Morning' again and went on his way, never knowing that he had dropped me a precious piece of information. Inquiry from another old man, hedging in a ditch, gave me the direction of Myrtle Cottage, a pretty little house, very trimly kept and with a very white doorstep.

My knocking remained unanswered, so I ventured round to the back, where, in a wash-house, a little apart from the cottage itself, a stout little woman, almost invisible in a cloud of steam, was lifting a number of plum-puddings out of a copper.

'Just a minute,' she called. 'One more. Eh, but they're hot, but then they've been boiling all day yesterday and all night. There now.' She dredged up the last pudding, put it beside the others, replaced the copper lid and turned to me. 'Well?'

'I'm sorry to stop you,' I said, 'but I understand that you had a Mrs. Meekin living with you in September.'

173

'That's right,' she replied, 'I did.'

'I knew her once years ago and only just heard that she was dead. I wondered whether you could tell me a little more about it.'

She looked at me rather doubtfully.

'Shouldn't you ought to go up to the Place? They're connections, you know.'

'I know. That's why I don't like to ask there. I don't want to remind them of their loss.' Really I didn't know I had it in me to be so crafty or to think up such good answers so quickly.

'Just as well,' she agreed. 'I happen to know that the lady took it very hard and the gentleman asked me not to talk about the dead lady. I went up there, you see, with a few bits and pieces that I had washed through for Mrs. Meekin. Well, there's not much I can tell you, but what I know you're welcome to. Look here, I was just going to make a cuppa tea. I allust do this time in the morning on account of Baker, that's my husband, getting off so early in the morning. I'm dry again by ten arter having my breakfast with him at six. Come in.'

She showed me into a neat and spotless little kitchen where a kettle was boiling over a stick fire and a brown teapot was warming on the hob. She made the tea, asked if I took milk and sugar and gave me an old-fashioned Pat-a-cake biscuit out of a bright red tin.

Once started, she proved to be a chatterbox, and I had no difficulty in finding out everything that she knew about her one-time lodger. It wasn't much. Antonia had only arrived two days before. She'd come from Sandborough, she'd said so. And directly she arrived she'd asked where the doctor lived and gone to see him. 'Poor thing, maybe she had an inkling that her time was short.' On the night of the tragedy she'd had a call on the telephone. Yes, Mrs. Baker had her own telephone—at least it wasn't hers really, it wasn't her name in the book, it belonged to her steady lodger, a young petrol man who was on holiday when Mrs. Meekin came. 'I told her that the best bedroom was his and that if she was there when he came back she'd have to move across the passage—him being steady, you see.' She'd asked about the telephone before she took the room. That and the bath were the main things. Well then, so this call had come and she'd come down out of her bath to answer it and then she'd gone back and dressed herself up very grand and asked Mrs. Baker to get Lorkin to bring his station taxi round for her and off she went. Never to return. Mr. Curwen had paid up, like the gentleman he was, to the end of the week, full board and everything. And he had taken away the trunk. Then Mrs. Baker herself had carried up the stockings and one or two bits of undies that Mrs. Meekin had asked her to wash for her. Mr. Curwen had met her and wanted to pay her, but that she wouldn't have.

'Did you happen to see Mrs. Curwen on that day?' I asked the question as carelessly as I could over the brim of my cup.

Yes, indeed she had, and hadn't it given her a turn? Hadn't she said, not thinking what she was saying, that if she'd met Mrs. Curwen at night and alone she would have run a mile and screamed her head off, taking her for the other poor lady's ghost? And hadn't that upset the lady so that Mr. Curwen had had to give her his arm and sign to Mrs. Baker to be quiet? And hadn't he told her later on that Mrs. Curwen was very sensitive and all about her likeness to her cousin and their mothers having been twins and all.

I accepted a second cup of tea and very welcome it was after the filth I had had for breakfast. Mrs. Baker chattered on, but nothing she now said was either new or important. I was soon able to rise and thank her warmly for telling me all that she had. She assured me that a chat was a pleasure but now she must stuff her turkey, her husband liked sage stuffing and the lodger, the steady, preferred chestnut, so she was going to make both and put it in at opposite ends. I left her to get on with it.

By this time I thought it better that I should not be out in the village any longer. Mr. Curwen or Miss Antonia might come into the place for something, and for me to be seen would give the whole game away.

I went back to my cold bedroom and wrapped the heavy, cotton-filled quilt that pretended to be an eiderdown round my knees and legs and scribbled down on a piece of paper what I felt I had gleaned.

Miss Antonia had come to the village on the very day that Miss Eloise and her husband had arrived.

She had insisted upon staying in a house with a telephone. She was *expecting* that invitation.

She had taken the trouble to establish a connection with the doctor. Was she *expecting* the 'heart attack'?

Although she was the laziest young woman I had ever met she had deliberately set out to walk the most difficult part of that little journey. Was that all part of the plot?

Mrs. Baker had tactlessly remarked upon her likeness to herself and she had been so upset that her 'husband' had been obliged to make explanations.

All those things pointed one way. The 'heart attack' had been Miss Eloise's and it was planned and timed to within —at most—twenty-four hours. And suddenly I knew—or thought I did. It was Miss Antonia's appearance which had caused Miss Eloise's heart attack. That was it. She had not expected to see her cousin: she had not seen her for four years, not since she had banished her from her house. Learning that that affair, which had caused her more pain than anyone except me knew, was not ended, but was

176

going on or beginning again, had caused her to fall into one of those fits of frenzy which had, for so long, taken toll of her health and energy. I had not been there to deal with it and she had died. Miss Antonia had taken her place.

A very probable story. That, or something very like it, had no doubt occurred. And although he was as directly responsible as though he had shot her or strangled her, no blame could be brought home to him. Oh, he was clever, there was no doubt of that. I had known that the moment I set eyes on him, that evening in the hall of the house in Merivale Avenue. Crafty and heartless, out for himself. He had always hated me because I saw through him.

I sat there and bitterly reproached myself for having accepted my dismissal. I should have insisted upon returning, seen Miss Eloise, judged for myself . . . and then I realised that by the time I received my notice it was already too late. She was dead, and by returning then I could have done no more than I was doing now.

Thus, thinking around and around the subject, I passed the hours. Even when I went downstairs again and ate some slices of leathery cold meat, cheered by the presence of the plate of two blackish potatoes, my mind was going in the same circles like a roundabout. At about a quarter to four Addy, whose name I had now learned was Mrs. Pratt, came and banged on my door. There was a change in her manner, she was almost servile.

'There's a gentleman to see you, ma'am. In fact there's two. I've put the parlour at your disposal and I'll have the fire going there in just a minute.'

Mr. Tickle, indeed, would have made a Red Russian respectful. He was a very tall thin old man with a great hooked nose and bright black eyes. The young man, his nephew, who accompanied him, was made on much the same lines. He insisted upon bringing in the fur-lined rug from his car and draping it around his uncle's chair. Then he announced his intention of returning to Notham and seeking what he called 'an hostelry.'

'If this,' he said, eyeing the smouldering fire, 'is a sample of St. Brodric's hospitality, I've seen enough of it. I'll be back by half-past six, Nunk. That do?'

'And now, Miss Plume,' said old Mr. Tickle when he had gone, 'will you sit down as close to that pathetic fire as you can and tell me everything from the very beginning?'

And very glad I was to do so. I went along slowly, telling everything that I knew, resisting the temptation to put in what I thought, beginning with my dismissal and ending with Mrs. Baker's story.

'Thank you,' he said when I had finished, 'you have done very well. And now perhaps we had better go and see the doctor.'

This time we were asked into the doctor's own sitting-room, where a good fire burned and I was able to get really warm for the first time since I had left London.

We went over everything again. It interested me to notice that although we were all three dealing with the same problem, we were taking different points of view, as different indeed as we were ourselves. Dr. Adams was worrying about the death certificate having been made out wrongly, though, as he pointed out, he had given it in good faith and no one would attach any blame to him. Still, he seemed to find it galling to think that he had fallen so completely into the trap that was laid for him. 'At my time of life, too,' he said, as though old age, instead of dulling his eyes and mind, should have been expected to sharpen them.

Mr. Tickle, on the other hand, was all concern for the money. He was much annoyed to think that this was Christmas Eve and that the next day and the next must pass before he could get in touch with the bank, to which cheques and what he called dividend certificates, bearing the forged signatures, had been sent.

Neither of these things worried me in the least. I just wanted to make sure that Mr. Curwen didn't enjoy the results of his crime. And I wanted that lying headstone taken up and Miss Eloise laid to rest properly with her christened name over her, ready for the Resurrection Day. And I wanted to know how and when and why exactly she had died.

Well, as I say, we talked it all over again and then Dr. Adams looked at his watch. 'We've time for a cup of tea,' he said, smiling at me, 'and then we'd better go into Notham and get into touch with the police.'

'And Miss Plume had better share the hostelry that my nephew is searching for,' said Mr. Tickle. 'For,' he added, looking at me, 'if our friend catches sight of you, he'll get warning and then ten to one he'll bolt. And that will mean more trouble for everybody.'

To prevent that happening I was willing to hide in a coal cellar.

Young Mr. Tickle returned with the news that the hostelry had been found, that there were fires lighted in the bedrooms and that dinner had been ordered. He helped his uncle into the long, low, boat-shaped car and swaddled him in the rug. He expressed regret that he could not offer me a lift as well, when he heard that I was also going to Notham. But after one look at that car I was glad to thank him and say that I was riding with Dr. Adams.

On the way I found courage to ask what I had been wanting to for hours.

'If the police take this up and find that what I say is true, would it be possible to have Miss Eloise up?'

'You mean exhumed? I suppose so. But I do not see that it would serve any useful purpose—that is, unless the identification muddle demands it.'

'It'd serve the purpose of relieving my mind,' I said firmly. 'The more I think of it the more I wonder. She died just *too* conveniently, just in the place and just at the time he wanted her to. Even if it was—no offence meant to you, Doctor—even if it *was* heart failure, it looks fishy to me. I'd like to have her up.'

He sighed a little wearily. 'If the whole of your story is true, Miss Plume, I'm bound to admit that I should too. If it's possible that I mistook one woman for another it's possible that I was even more deceived. Dear me, I've been thinking for some time that I ought to retire. Now I'm beginning to be sure of it.' He sighed again and the car groaned as if it sympathised with him, as I did.

'I shouldn't take this affair as proof of that,' I said as cheerfully as possible. 'You were meant to be deceived, and Mr. Curwen is very clever.'

'But not clever enough to deceive you, eh, Miss Plume? Not clever enough for that.'

'He never deceived me for a moment,' I said, and that was the truth. 'And I shan't rest until the whole world sees him as clearly as I do.'

And after that we were silent until we reached the town and stopped before a large building and, looking out, I saw a light illuminating the word 'Police.'

Richard Curwen

OSCAR WILDE—or, if not he, some other juggler with words—says somewhere, 'Revenge is a kind of rude justice.' Sitting here, alone, with everything over and nothing to do but to think, I brood over those words. I am bound to admit that Emma Plume, in her desire to avenge Eloise, has brought about a form of rude justice. How rude! And yet how just!

I can't help it, it makes me laugh. Every time I think of it I laugh. I wonder sometimes whether they think I am crazy. The doctor seems to visit me a lot—but maybe that is usual. Maybe I am 'under observation.'

But I don't feel crazy. Though that means nothing. I remember reading somewhere that one of the signs of insanity is to be perfectly sure that you are the one sane person in an insane world. I feel sane enough. I just sit here and think. I give no trouble. I never look at the books which are allowed me for the distraction of my mind; I do not welcome the visits of either the governor or the padre. I just sit here and think. And when I reach the point of my thinking where I realise again why I am where I am, I burst out laughing. And then, sooner or later the warder looks in and presently the doctor appears. Occasionally he tests my reflexes. I cross my legs at his request and he bangs my knees with a little rubber mallet. He flashes a torch into my eyes. He seems vaguely disappointed when I flinch and jerk in the normal manner. I suppose he feels that anyone who can find amusement in the situation that I am in *ought* to register abnormal reactions.

For very soon now I am going to hang. I am going to hang by the neck until I am dead, for the murder of Eloise, my wife. That is the rude justice. But the method they ascribe to me—that is what makes me laugh.

I go all over it again.

We had a very good Christmas, the first and the last. It was very quiet, just Antonia, Diana and me. We were set on giving the child a good time, partly because we had certain qualms about ridding ourselves of her so soon. We had all the usual foolish things: holly and mistletoe and over-crammed stockings at the foot of the bed. We had a Christmas tree, which I rather enjoyed decorating. I used only silver things, icicles and stars and tinsel, and all the parcels were packed in silver paper. It looked like a frozen tree from a remote Northern forest. There was something Valse Triste-ish about it, like dancing in a hall of ice. We pulled crackers and wore ridiculous hats and burned raisins in brandy in the darkness of the hall.

For the greater part of the day Diana behaved better than usual, though she completely ignored the present which Antonia had given her, a really beautiful doll, like a Hawaiian girl, and went about all day clutching the old-fashioned doll which had come from Emma Plume, complete with flannel petticoat carefully herring-boned. Antonia and I had laughed over that and Antonia said, 'Obviously Nanny has never heard of step-ins!' And all the time Emma Plume was . . .

We were just about all set to leave Moat House. Antonia and I were going first to Juan les Pins for a month and then

184

from Marseilles, joining a cruise which was going through the Suez to Ceylon and Singapore, on to Australia, back via the Pacific Islands, through Panama and home by the West Indies. Antonia was wildly excited. The prospect of leaving the Moat House, which she hated, and of being able to cast off the memory of Eloise completely, sent her into a mood of gaiety and nonsense which caught me up in it and made life deliriously pleasurable. Never were preparations made and trunks packed so light-heartedly. This, we felt, was how we were intended to live, this was how we were meant to love.

Into this paradise there burst the devil in the shape of a detective-sergeant with a warrant for my arrest. There were two charges, obtaining money by false pretences and causing a false registration of death.

We, that is Antonia and I, gave the law no help. In the face of a veritable 'cloud of witnesses' we tried to brazen it out. It was Antonia who had died and was buried; it was Eloise who was my wife and who had signed the cheques and the dividend receipts. But, of course, it was hopeless. The dentist who had removed Eloise's teeth; the doctor who had stitched her wrist where the cat had bitten her; the tailor who had cut her hideously expensive suits and could prove that her arms were two inches longer than Antonia's and her shoulders three inches narrower; the man who had fitted her long sixes in shoes (Antonia wore short fives); and a handwriting specialist who proved by graphs and measurements and photography that the signatures written after a certain date differed from all but five of those written earlier: all these people combined to condemn me. There were also the people who had known both Eloise and Antonia, chief amongst them, of course, the infernal Emma Plume.

Side by side Antonia and I fought to the last; but it was quite hopeless. It had been hopeless since the moment

185

when the first suspicion shot through that woman's mind. I got seven years; Antonia, for helping me, six months. Her defence put in some good word for her by pleading that she was entirely dominated by me. The turn in affairs had completely altered Antonia; she was older and graver, and she gave me the surprise of my life by sending me a message that she would wait for me.

Seven years, I thought, would dwindle to five or five and a half if I behaved myself impeccably. And although I was full of bitterness and disappointment, I set myself resolutely to bear the immediate future with patience and resignation. I should still be a comparatively young man when I emerged from prison. I should still be under forty, young enough to begin to prove to Antonia, if she kept her word to me, that I was willing to work as well as to scheme for her. I had altered too. God, how that makes me laugh! Talk about a reformative influence!

I was quite unmoved to hear that, owing to certain peculiarities in the case, Eloise's body was to be exhumed. Let them exhume her, I thought, they'll do a very unpleasant job for the sake of very little information. Eloise died because she was frightened, and fright leaves no trace.

After all, it was never the killing which had had to be concealed. From the moment that Antonia had set foot in the house and the change of identity accomplished, the body had been there for anyone to see. As I had said on that night, the whole medical faculty could have examined it and drawn no dangerous conclusion. 'Where,' asks someone in a Chesterton story, 'would a wise man hide a leaf?' The answer is, 'In a forest.' And that thought should govern the removal of any unwanted person: let the confirmed alcoholic die of delirium tremens, let the woodcarver slit a vital artery in his wrist, let the neurotic die of fright, and what will an exhumation prove? Nothing.

So at least I thought, settling down to wait my time

without worry or repining, so that I might emerge with my hair the right colour and no unnecessary lines upon my face.

Time passed. Eminent and earnest scientists in London brooded over Eloise's poor remains.

This is the funny part, this is what makes me laugh every time I think about it. This is what amuses me. They found that Eloise was chock-full of Morphaline, a form of morphia that remains in the body after death and is taken during life to induce sleep.

So I am going to hang—not because at a certain time, in a certain place, in certain circumstances, I put a certain piece of graven wax beneath the steel point of a needle. I am going to hang because Eloise, that Blessed Damozel, that faery child, my wife, the woman whom I knew so well that I could kill her with a thought, had all unknown to me been a dope fiend.

Isn't it funny? Isn't it the century's prime jest? Can you wonder that I laugh?

And I helped to hang myself because I made a fool-proof plan; because I forgot nothing.

In the famous tradition of English justice I received a scrupulously fair trial. The fact that I had been proved guilty of using Eloise's money and passing off Antonia as my wife came out afresh in the course of it, but was not a premise.

As they wove, out of my arrangements, out of all the bits that went to make up the plan, the strong rope to hang me by, I had two hopes. I hoped that the indefatigable police, who will leave no stone unturned, might happen upon the person from whom Eloise had obtained her supplies. And I hoped that somebody would come forward and remember and mention that he or she had seen the drug in Eloise's possession. Both hopes were vain. Eloise had had money, she had been able to command what she wanted, secrecy. And she had undoubtedly been the most crafty and clever schemer in the world.

There was just one person who knew, who must have known, and that was Emma Plume. That is humorous too! To think that after all these years of mutual hatred and distrust we should meet in such circumstances, I with hope in my heart, she with obdurate hatred.

Obdurate! Nothing would shake her. She had known Miss Eloise with the greatest possible intimacy for eighteen years, and she had never, never, never seen or heard or suspected anything that might point to her having been a drug addict. Again and again the defence returned to that point—it was in fact the only one where any progress could be hoped for—had she never noticed unusual lassitude, drowsiness, unequal spirits? Never, replied Emma Plume. Except when Miss Eloise was upset by something or somebody, she was the most placid and even-tempered person ever born. There was nothing in her life, nothing, with which Emma Plume was not cognisant. It was impossible for her to have taken so much as an aspirin without Emma Plume's knowledge.

Hell consume the hag, she must have known that she was lying. She couldn't have lived in Eloise's pocket like that and not known. Or even if that were possible she should have been willing to admit that this new revelation made everything about Eloise as plain as print. Every fit and faint, the little gaieties, the sudden depressions, every tantrum and collapse now lay wholly explained, bare and simple proof that she had, over a long period of time, had recourse to a drug.

But nothing could pry such an admission out of Emma Plume. And from the prosecution's point of view she was the best witness anyone could hope for. Soberly dressed, exuding respectability from every pore, reeking with honesty, loyalty and common sense. Even her damned level unemphatic countrified voice carried conviction and helped to hang me. Now and then, when she spoke of Eloise, it deepened and broke upon a note of emotion. She even staged a telling little breakdown, when she burst out with something about robbing the poor lady of her life and her headstone and now trying to take away her reputation. She had the jury in the hollow of her hand from the first moment. And she meant to hang me. From the instant that she knew that Eloise was dead she meant to hang me.

And of course, in addition to her unshakable evidence, there was all the damning story of my activities up to and after the fatal day. Every tiny ramification of my scheme was brought into the light and considered: Antonia's visit to old Adams; the absence of servants; the dismissal of Emma Plume; even the present that I had given to Bob Soames in order to enable him to marry Alice. They discovered everything except the thing that would have helped me—the source of Eloise's supplies. And of course there was a sort of rough justice in that. All the precautions that I had taken in order to commit killing by frightening were construed into proof that I had killed by poisoning. What could be fairer?

And then the police, who couldn't find where Eloise had got her Morphaline, discovered two tablets in the bathroom cabinet at Moat Place. I swear I had never noticed them.

Antonia—who had been turning steadily against me ever since the exhumation—now gave me a surprise by claiming them for her own. I believe that she meant well. But it was the final mistake, the last link. Up till then there had at least been no evidence of where I had—or might have—obtained the stuff. And if she had said, what was obviously the truth, that she had found them there amongst Eloise's things when she took up residence, I might be in a very different position at this moment. But no, misguided and perhaps in an attempt to make amends for the harm that her other evidence had done me, Antonia must say that the stuff was hers. Very well then, had she had it at Sandborough? Yes. And had the accused had access to her possessions at Sandborough? I was surprised to learn how many people knew exactly how often and upon what an intimate footing I had visited Antonia at The Flitch. That clinched it. *Why* I had done it had always been plain, now *how* was solved. I don't think anybody in England had the slightest doubt of my guilt.

After all, why should they? I did it. Without my intervention Eloise would probably at this moment be throwing a fit somewhere and gaining a lot of sympathy to which she was not entitled and I should be yelling for Nanny.

Once or twice, when I saw that there was no hope, I had a mischievous impulse to say, 'If you look in the locked cupboard on the stairs—and you probably haven't overlooked that—you will find, or have found, a nice new gramophone with Rechzof's Gypsy Dance for four violins still in position. That is the lethal weapon, one quite unique, I believe.'

But that wouldn't profit me and anyway they would take that as just a fairy tale. And maybe some time there'll be some other poor bastard who will think of getting rid of an unwanted woman that way. I'd hate to scotch his chances, though naturally I wouldn't hesitate for that if I thought it'd help me now.

So I'll go down in the crime books as a common poisoner. And probably Mr. Roughead will live to amuse people with the story as he has often enough amused me with others. It will be, as I told Antonia, a good story: remote house named Moat Place, crazy wife and beautiful mistress. But the secret of it will never be told. I know one half and Eloise the other. And dead men tell no tales. Every time when I think of Eloise's final trick on me I laugh. . . .

But now and again I stop thinking that way. I think instead of tomorrow and tomorrow, some unknown day that is coming towards me on soundless and relentless feet. On that day I shall hang. Because I was poor and loved Antonia, and would not be resigned, and because Emma Plume hated me, I shall hang. I think of the bolt and the noose, the pinions and the shrouded face. Somewhere there is a man who is working out a mathematical calculation about my weight and the length of drop I shall need.

He is working for my death as I worked for Eloise's.

There is coming a grey dawn when I shall be alone and terrified as Eloise was alone and terrified.

I shall be helpless, as she was.

She never harmed me, any more than I have harmed the man who will despatch me. Sometimes our fates seem to have been so inextricably woven that I even feel a sort of fellow-feeling for her. And that makes me laugh too.

But on that morning I shall probably not laugh. I may scream, as she did. Occasionally now when I am not laughing I scream. The memory of the trial comes upon me and I laugh. The anticipation of the final moment follows and I scream. Between whiles I just think. I sit here and think —of Antonia, whom I loved with a love that did neither of us any good; of Eloise, who tricked me so finely; of Emma Plume with her implacable hatred. It's a funny story.

I realise that I have wasted my life. There were many small things that I enjoyed, hot baths, clean linen, idling in the sun, good food. Small things that I sacrificed for their own continuance and for Antonia. Perhaps there were things that Eloise enjoyed too. Why do I say *perhaps?* I know that there were. I cut her off from them. That has occurred to me lately. Many things have. And sometimes when something strikes me suddenly I cry out and beat my head against the wall; and that makes me think of Eloise beating her head. I understand now.

191

They do not, here, look upon me with the distaste with which I used to regard Eloise. Everybody is very kind. They try to distract my mind; offer me pleasant food for the sustenance of a body that has really ceased to exist. Generally I refuse it; and I think it will be a lie if they make the usual report, 'The dead man ate a hearty breakfast.'